Daughters of Zelophehad

WYNELL BROOKS HUTSON

authorHOUSE®

AuthorHouse™
1663 Liberty Drive, Suite 200
Bloomington, IN 47403
www.authorhouse.com
Phone: 1-800-839-8640

First published by AuthorHouse 1/9/2008

ISBN: 978-1-4343-5293-4 (sc)

Library of Congress Control Number: 2007909912

Printed in the United States of America
Bloomington, Indiana

This book is printed on acid-free paper.

Acknowledgments

People who read my first novel *Assignment Precious Cargo* kept asking me if I intended to write another. Well, I really didn't intend to write the first. It was just something I felt compelled to do. Now I'm glad I did.

But their questions set me to thinking about another possible subject, and I remembered scripture I first encountered years ago that intrigued me—two or three short passages in the Old Testament that told about five Israelite women—even gave their names. They were sisters. That caught my attention because I had five sisters.

I have heard it said one should write about what one knows—well, I know sisters and I have studied the Bible for years. Each time I came to these women in my reading through the Bible I would wonder what they were like. When I began to consider writing about them, I decided I would just make them like my sisters and tell how I think things might have happened to bring them to what little is told in the Bible.

It has been hard work—but great fun—to write this story. But once I assigned one of the Bible names to a sister, I used her personality for that character and that made it flow. Of course, I couldn't make their lives exactly fit the lives of my sisters, but I believe I captured them well.

So, I am dedicating the story to them. To: Carrie Frederick, Anita Pugh, Nina Boyles, Natalie Sanderson, and Donna Roeder—quite a quintet of characters.

Foreword

In the time before God sent his Son to die for our sins, before The Comforter, the Holy Spirit, was sent to indwell the hearts of Believers, in the time when The People were newly under The Law, they had to deal with the same trials we experience today. The Holy Spirit only came upon a certain person at a certain time to enable him to perform the specific task that God assigned him to perform.

Women in most cultures of that time had no rights; they belonged to men as chattel—houses, land, animals, etc. But in The Exodus we begin to see how Jehovah changes their status. The women of Israel begin to come into their own.

Could it be that the God some accuse of prejudice against women was the instigator of Women's Rights? You decide for yourself. Herein is the story of five women in the long journey of wandering in the wilderness after Israel refused to enter the land God had given them.

It is the story of the five daughters of Zelophehad we first encounter in Numbers 26:33 and 27:1-7, and again in the whole chapter of Numbers 36, and lastly in Joshua 17:1-4. The Bible doesn't say it happened this way; this is only what I have imagined. But it might have happened this way. It could have happened this way.

Chapter 1

The pillar of cloud—the Glory of God—stood steadfastly before the thousands of tents of Israel. The sun shone brightly upon them. Could one have viewed them from above, one would have seen a huge cross—the formation in which the tents were set up surrounding the tabernacle.

Judah, Issachar, and Zebulun on the east; Reuben, Simeon, and Gad on the south; Ephraim, Benjamin, and Manasseh on the west, and Dan, Asher, and Naphtali on the north.

There had been a gentle breeze earlier in the day, but as Zelophehad entered his tent on the very outer edge of the camp, it seemed there was not one breath of air to be had in the whole of the wilderness.

There, on one of the straw mats used for sleeping, lay Naronah, his wife, pale and still and beautiful in death. Beside her, the attending women had placed the body of the child to which she had given birth that morning.

It was a male child. He was perfectly formed in every way, but he, too, was pale and still and dead.

Zelophehad fell to his knees and let out a cry that split the surrounding silence, "Oh, God of Israel! Forgive me!" The anguish in the cry was so palpable it rent the hearts of his five daughters who huddled together at the side of the tent.

Mahlah, the oldest, felt faint, but kept an arm firmly around her youngest sister and she sank in a heap in the dust of the tent floor to weep for her mother. Little Tirzah put her arms around Mahlah and patted her in an effort to comfort her.

Noah walked to where her father had fallen. Her eyes were blazing with anger. She could hardly restrain herself; she wanted to spit upon him. "You see what your unfairness has brought about! All she ever wanted in her whole life was to please you. How could you have treated her so?"

This question brought gasps from the women attending the two bodies.

1

Noah's mouth contorted this way and that as she strove as to keep back tears and more bitterness. Zelophehad did not move or give indication that he heard his second daughter's words. She stood over him, straight and slim and tall. Her graceful hands which were very brown from being in the sun day after day, opened and closed into fists several times before she burst into tears and ran out of the tent.

She ran back to the sheep to share her anger and grief with her charges.

Hoglah had stepped up behind her sister as she stood over their weeping father. Her expression was enigmatic. She had reached out to Noah just as the older girl wheeled and ran. Hoglah paused to search the faces of the women who stood silently waiting along the far side if the tent. Her expression did not change as she followed her sister out into the hot, still afternoon.

This left only Milcah, a bewildered nine year-old, standing alone, straining to make some sort of sense out of this tragedy—understanding with a wisdom beyond her years the positions and actions of her family.

She kept her eyes on her father who appeared to be completely crushed at the loss of his beloved wife. Milcah remembered the stories her mother told of him in happier days. He had never shown any affection to her or to Tirzah. But Mahlah, Noah, and Hoglah spoke often of the joyful times when their father had laughed and played with them—and had openly showed his love and respect for their beautiful mother.

Milcah had tried to imagine him as a happy, loving father, but just couldn't reconcile that picture with the man he had been since she could remember. She had etched in her heart the memory of a time three years ago when the girls' mother had told them of her great love for their father and his even greater love for her.

Milcah remembered the tender look in her mother's eyes as she related to her daughters the beauty of this love and her words, "I only pray that each of you finds a love even half so wonderful. It is something that will sustain you whatever else may come to you in life."

Milcah had been only six years old and had no real understanding of it at the time, but Naronah did get it across to all of them (with the exception of Tirzah who was hardly more than a toddler) that she and their father had a very special love.

Milcah believed it. The grown-ups around them believed it. She heard remarks from them from time to time expressing wonder at the relationship and speculating about the fact that Zelophehad would not take another wife to produce sons for him—a thing which was all important to a man of Israel.

The absence of an heir hung over their lives like a dark cloud and had finally resulted in today's tragedy. It was present there now, shedding a pall over the atmosphere in their richly appointed tent.

Zelophehad's weeping finally subsided and then ended abruptly. He rose to his feet and addressed the women who had stood quietly by, allowing him to collect himself.

"What happened to my wife and her son?"

Hasenuah, his sister-in-law, stepped forward from the group to answer. "We believe Amalekites killed them. From the appearance of the wound, Naronah was run through with a spear and the little boy still had an arrow in him when we found them."

Zelophehad shuddered when she spoke of the spear and winced when he heard his long-awaited son had been brutally stabbed with an arrow.

"What have you done with the arrow?"

The women looked at one another and then all around the tent. "It's disappeared," one of them told him. "It was set apart over on that basket." She pointed and continued looking around the room. "I don't know what could have happened to it."

The rest of the women also seemed to be mystified. *What would anyone want with an Amalekite arrow? Why should anyone take it?*

Zelophehad then asked them, "Why is my tent on the edge of the camp?" They hung their heads and did not answer. "Did you not hear me? Why is my tent so far out of its position in our tribe's order of march?"

Seeing the women did not want to answer him, Milcah said, "Father, we just could not keep up with the rest." She stepped back a pace when her father scowled at her. "Couldn't keep up?" He was incredulous. Milcah stood her ground—she was telling him the truth.

"The men you left to help us went away after the first day. Then it was only Asriel, Epher, and Shechem with Mother; Mahlah, Noah, Hoglah, and me and little Tirzah left to drive the livestock and tend the donkeys and oxcarts carrying the tent, and then set it up when the cloud halted."

"Mother started having her pains," added Mahlah, who had raised herself from the dust and was wiping her eyes, trying to end her tears. "We had to rearrange the baggage and get her into one of the carts. That threw us further behind."

"Oh God—my poor Naronah," Zelophehad whispered.

"We barely got the tent set up in time for the baby to be born," Mahlah went on. "I sent Hoglah to bring women to see to Mother while my sisters and I helped the young men get the livestock settled in and fed and watered.

"They said Mother had a very easy delivery with no problems, so they left her alone with the baby for an hour or so while they went to check on their families. They came back later to find Hasenuah had returned early and found Mother and the baby dead." Mahlah began to cry again.

Tirzah was crying, too, looking at the still body of the woman who had given her all the attention she could afford to give in an effort to compensate for a father who completely ignored her except for giving her an order for work now and then. She turned from Mahlah and went to her mother's body and lay down next to it, reaching her little arm across the cold breast, trying to embrace her.

Zelophehad's eyes followed her and he reached down and removed the little arm from Naronah's shoulder and lifted Tirzah bodily away from her mother as if removing an unwanted animal. "Here," he said to Mahlah, as he set Tirzah down beside her again. "We must start to make arrangements to bury them. I want to have my son, Oni, circumcised before he is laid away, so we had better take care of that today and we'll bury them tomorrow morning."

Milcah went to her little sister and hugged her close to take the sting out of their father's cold gesture.

The four women who had been standing by exchanged looks when Zelophehad mentioned circumcision. "Why do that to the poor little baby?" Hasenuah began.

"He has to be circumcised!" insisted Zelophehad. "He has to be every bit a son of Abraham before I put him in the ground."

"But can we find someone who can do this?" Hasenuah knew that the circumcised generation who had come out of Egypt was rapidly dying off.

Zelophehad said impatiently, "I'm sure there are still many who can do it. Now I want one found as quickly as possible."

All but one of the women left the tent. Hasenuah stayed to try to help the man who once might have been her husband. "Brother," she said, "lie down and rest while we are waiting, and Mahlah and I will prepare some food for you and the ones who attend the circumcision."

"No," was the stern answer, "all who have touched the dead bodies are unclean, and so will everyone who comes into this tent.

"Mahlah, take Milcah and Tirzah and go help whoever is tending the cattle and sheep. None of us will eat until after we've buried them early in the morning. Then, after we have all been cleansed, I will find and hire more servants so we can keep pace if the pillar of cloud should start to move."

Mahlah stared at her father who was acting as if nothing had happened.

"Go!" he said.

She took the girls by their hands and hurried off to find Noah, Hoglah, and their cousins, the young men who helped with their father's livestock.

Zelophehad paced as he waited for the women to return with a circumciser.

Hasenuah sat down on the rug spread along the side of the tent and watched him. She still had great admiration for this man. She was amazed at his sudden shift from uncontrolled weeping to this business-like attitude with not a hint of the loss of the overpowering love she knew had ruled his whole life—the love that had actually ruined his life for the last eighteen years.

Within the space of an hour, the women returned with an old man who only performed the ceremonial act asked of him after protesting he did not think it right to circumcise a dead person.

Zelophehad assured him that he, himself, would accept the consequences should there be any. When it was done, he paid the man with a silver coin and thanked the women, sending them all away protesting.

Then he went back to the poor little body they had rewrapped in swaddling clothes, picked it up, and held it to his breast, and wept again for his son and for his one and only love.

Chapter 2

Asriel sat upon a rock on the outside edge of the Israelite camp. He had found just the spot to sit and watch the flock of Zelophehad, his kinsman. And there was also a tree. It was stunted, but nonetheless, an actual tree, and there was grass and other plants for the sheep to feed upon.

The grass that they always found in the places where the pillar of cloud halted was a matter of wonder to this young shepherd. This was such a stark and barren land in which they wandered. But, as surely as the manna was always there in the morning for the people, the grass was always there for the animals—and also a place to water them.

Asriel had heard the stories of the murmuring and complaining of the people when they first came out of Egypt—how Jehovah in many miraculous ways had produced water, over and over, fit for them to drink.

He especially liked to hear the older men speak of the time Moses led The People to Marah. It was just after God had brought them across the Red Sea. After three days of traveling and finding no water, they came upon this beautiful place of trees and grass and waters bubbling up into pools wherever one looked.

Then someone made the startling discovery that all this water was bitter and not fit for the Israelites or their animals. The people became furious; their water had run out and here they were with abundant water in view, but it was water that would hurt instead of help. They turned on Moses once again and Moses turned to the LORD, as always before.

The LORD then showed Moses a tree and told Moses to cast it into the waters. Moses obeyed and the waters were instantly healed and became sweet and drinkable! Every time this story was told, someone else had to tell about the rock in Horeb. This was a time when the people had journeyed from the Wilderness of Sin and had made camp in Rephidim—and once again there was no water.

The whole camp began to cry out against Moses, accusing him of deliberately bringing them out of Egypt in order to kill them and their cattle with thirst. And the crowd was growing angrier by the minute. Moses turned to the only source of help—the LORD.

The LORD told him to take in his hand the rod with which he had divided the Red Sea and to take the elders of Israel with him. He instructed Moses that He, the LORD, would stand there upon the rock in Horeb. He then told Moses to strike the rock with the rod in the sight of the elders and water would come out of it for the people to drink.

Once again Moses was obedient and the water gushed forth from the rock—water for thousands and thousands of people and thousands of their livestock. It was a never- ending, ever-flowing stream of pure, clear, life-sustaining water.

Asriel, the shepherd, was sitting cross-legged upon his rock, turning this pleasant picture over and over in his mind when he caught sight of someone running toward him from between the tents. He jumped down quickly and retrieved his rod which he had left leaning against the rock.

People on the outskirts of the camp were obliged to be always alert. Amalekite raiders might turn up at any time. These cowards hoped to find one or two alone and kill them to take whatever loot they might without a real fight.

But this was certainly no raider. He immediately recognized his beautiful cousin, Noah. When she reached him he could tell she had been crying, but she was trying hard to compose her self.

"What is wrong, Noah?" he asked.

"My mother and my baby brother have been killed!"

"Killed? How? Who would kill your dear, sweet mother?" Asriel couldn't believe what he was hearing. "I thought everything was going so well when you left us the second time to see how she was doing."

Noah leaned against the rock with her head bowed. "The women left her alone because she was doing so well and they were only gone for an hour or so. They think the Amalekites killed her and the baby."

"Amalekites?" Asriel found this hard to believe. "But how did they get into the camp without someone seeing them? I have been here with your father's sheep. Epher and Shechem are yonder with the rest of the livestock. My father and uncles and their herdsmen are next to us, and then the others. The Amalekites would have had to come through part of the camp to get to your mother."

"But they did; they killed her and that sweet baby. Asriel, you are forgetting how far out of our place we were because we got so far behind."

"Does your father know? Has he come back?"

"Yes," Noah answered. "Someone went to tell him and he is in the tent now. He was not far away. He had been with the Reubenites negotiating for another wife—and my poor mother knew it. He told her before he left. He wouldn't believe her when she promised the baby would be a man-child. He just left her when she needed him most."

Asriel was astonished to hear these bitter words pouring from the mouth of his beloved cousin. It was so unlike her. She was always a joy to be around. Her beauty alone made one happy, but she had such an agreeable disposition—always looking forward—always finding things to laugh about and share with others.

Noah was the real reason Asriel had agreed to work for his uncle, Zelophehad. His own father, Machir, had plenty of help and Zelophehad paid generously, but the work was actually enjoyable when he was working with Noah. He loved her and so did everyone who knew her.

He was struggling to find words to help and comfort her when he saw another figure walking aimlessly from the camp. Asriel also recognized this one, even though her actions were strange and foreign to her usual demeanor.

"Noah, look at Hoglah. What is she doing?"

The girl had been ambling toward them, but stopped and started back toward the tents. She stopped the second time and stared toward them. After a few seconds she began to walk toward the cattle and other livestock their cousins were tending. As Noah looked up, Hoglah turned toward her and Asriel once again. She took only a few steps and then sat down on the rocky ground.

"There's something wrong with her!" Asriel asserted.

Noah didn't answer him, but started to run toward her sister. When Noah came near, the younger girl looked up and smiled and held out her hand. She had a strange look in her eyes; her whole attitude seemed strange to Noah.

"What are you doing, Hoglah?"

"I was coming to find you, but I started thinking maybe I should run away and hide."

"Why should you want to hide?"

"Someone killed my mother and her baby boy."

"And that made you think you need to hide?" Noah couldn't make the connection.

"I'm afraid they'll find out I saw."

"You saw! You saw the Amalekites kill our mother?"

"No," Hoglah's head jerked suddenly and she said in a completely different tone, "No, I didn't see anything, Noah. I was coming to help with the sheep so Asriel could go help Shechem and Epher water the stock and settle them into the common place with the uncles' animals." She looked back toward the tents. "Here comes Mahlah and she's bringing the girls with her. We'll have plenty of help getting the sheep ready for the night," she said.

Mahlah came hurrying toward them leading Tirzah by the hand. It was difficult for the grieving little one to keep pace. Milcah followed close behind. Mahlah stopped beside Hoglah and said, "Get up sister and come along. Father says we are to let Asriel go to help Epher and Shechem with the livestock. We are to get the sheep to a common fold and settled in for the night."

As she started on toward Asriel and the sheep, pushing Tirzah along, she told her and Milcah, "Run to the other side and start them toward us. We'll take them to Uncle Joseph's and Machir's flocks. Noah, you must spend the night with them."

By this time they had nearly reached Asriel. He had watched them all the way. *How alike and how different were his cousins Mahlah and Noah. They were both slim and about the same height. Both pretty, but different in a way he could not define.* Mahlah had always had health problems, but managed to work and be a great help to her mother with the household chores around their tent. She considered herself second in command in their home and was always instructing her sisters as to what work they should do.

Mahlah's skin was lighter because most of her work was inside. Noah was darker because she was in the sun every day. Her father worked her and Hoglah as he would sons—and in the past year had begun to train Milcah in the same way.

Zelophehad had more than three times as many sheep and cattle and goats and donkeys as his brothers. He was the oldest son and had received the greater inheritance. His father, Hepher, had owned some livestock in Egypt, but he had also successfully spoiled his Egyptian neighbors who had been more than willing to give generously to the Israelites to get them to leave their country so their god, Jehovah, would end his terrible judgments upon them and their land.

Hepher had also obtained riches in silver, gold, gems, and in many other forms from the desperate Egyptians. So, although Zelophehad had no sons he had more than ample funds to hire workers. His animals faithfully reproduced and the other tribes who had less livestock than Reuben, Gad, and Manasseh regularly purchased what was needed from their kinsmen—increasing their wealth and also their work.

The daughters of Zelophehad worked as hard as any Israelite in the camp, man or woman. They had very little time to make themselves attractive, but Asriel thought their beauty was second to none. Many others agreed.

Asriel stood awaiting the instructions he knew would be coming from Mahlah. He grinned at Noah, hoping for the responding grin he usually received when Mahlah was telling them what to do. Noah didn't respond. She was watching Hoglah with concern. Hoglah's face had a look she had never seen before—a haunted expression, yet almost blank.

Mahlah said, "Father sent us to help. I think we should get the sheep rounded up for the night. Noah will stay with them. You go and help Epher and Shechem. You can decide who gets the night watch.

"Father is going to bury Mother and the little boy in the morning. Then we'll all have to be cleansed and our tent will have to be cleansed." She paused.

"He sent for a man to come and circumcise our little brother! I can't believe all this is happening!" She sat down and began to cry again. "Go on, Asriel, she said, "we'll take care of the sheep."

Chapter 3

Zelophehad finally placed his little son's body in the hollow made between the forearm and shoulder of his wife when the women had crossed her arms over her breast. In this manner he would place them in the grave.

He stared into her dear face once again remembering how their marriage came to be. Zelophehad's parents had picked a wife for him from the daughters of a wealthy man of the tribe of Reuben. It would have been a "brilliant" match—bringing more riches and influence to the family.

The girl's name was Hasenuah. She was pretty and intelligent and seemed to be quite an agreeable person. But their son, Zelophehad, had been in love with someone else since he was a small boy. That someone was Naronah. He was not only in love, but he was completely taken and captivated with her. She was not as pretty in the conventional way as Hasenuah; her family was neither rich nor influential. And she was two years older than Zelophehad but had never considered another boy since they first saw each other when she was ten and he was eight years old. There was just this magical connection between them that no one could break.

Zelophehad had always been an obedient son in every aspect of life. He enjoyed a great relationship with his parents. He was their oldest son and he was the example for his brothers.

But when his parents told him of the match they had made for him to marry Hasenuah, he flatly refused. Threats did not budge him—offers of incentive made no impression. He was adamant. He would marry no one but Naronah.

When he ran to tell her of what was going on with his parents, he learned she had twice suffered through the same controversy. Two of her younger sisters had ended up betrothed to her would-be husbands. And here she was—unmarried at the advanced age of twenty years—a shame and a disgrace to her unhappy parents.

So Zelophehad's father took a cue from Naronah's parents and claimed the offered bride for his second son (who was named Joseph, after his great, great, great, grandfather). Zelophehad then was allowed to claim Naronah from her relieved parents and all seemed satisfied. The two young lovers were deliriously happy as physical love was added to their already wonderful and special relationship

Within a year they had produced a child. It was a girl child but, nonetheless, a beautiful, healthy girl child, and they named her Mahlah. They showered her with love and thanked the God of Israel for her and went about trying to produce another child—a male child. This was all-important to an Israelite.

A family must have sons! Sons to prove the father's virility—sons to complete the mother's purpose in life; sons to help with the work of the father—sons to carry on his name; sons to add to the strength of the family and of their tribe; sons to fight the enemies and to protect the people. And any son born to a woman of Israel might turn out to be the "seed" promised to Eve, the one who would bruise the serpent's head! Two days after Mahlah was born, Hasenuah delivered a son to Joseph, Zelophehad's younger brother, and she thought, *See, Zelophehad, I am more worthy than your precious, special love, Naronah. I gave your brother a son.*

But Zelophehad and Naronah were even happier than before; there was plenty of time for sons. Soon Naronah was carrying another child. This time she was sure it was a boy. And it was a boy—a beautiful child—only born much too soon to survive. Naronah had cried and asked Zelophehad to forgive her. He had comforted her and asked how he could blame her for something over which she had no control. And they went on living and enjoying each other and their daughter—and trying for a son.

Another son came, but too early again. At the time they were burying this second son, Hasenuah presented Joseph with a second son, hale and healthy.

At the times when the family gathered, Hasenuah didn't exactly flaunt the fact that she could produce sons, but in little subtle ways she made sure that the man who had rejected her noted that she had already given his brother two sons. She was superior to his beloved wife, Naronah.

He noted the fact, but he could not imagine being married to anyone other than his true love; and they were not unhappy when her next pregnancy produced the beautiful little Noah—a complete joy from the day she was born.

The next year, and the next, brought miscarriages of sons. Now it was beginning to create a strain in the relationship, but their love was so strong that it held fast. Zelophehad's father and uncles had begun to urge him to take a second wife after the first two sons had been born and died. He could not bring himself to it. They shook their heads in amazement that he loved Naronah enough to bare the shame of having no son.

"Why, you could even divorce her for this," his father had told him. He had no desire to divorce her. He loved her more than anything in life, but he wanted a son and the burden grew heavier as the years passed.

Then Hoglah was born and somehow he had managed to stay happy and keep a pleasant atmosphere in their home. But when the next two pregnancies produced girls, he seemed to lose hope and also to lose the desire to keep trying for his heir.

Zelophehad had looked around him and wondered why God was withholding from them the blessing of having an heir and other male children. Joseph already had five sons; his other brothers had sons.

Naronah did everything she could to please him. She kept herself looking beautiful and desirable. He knew, for she told him over and over, that she wanted a son as much as he. It was a matter of shame to her that she had been unable to give him a son, but she was fiercely proud of her daughters. She held her head up among the women who looked down upon her and openly praised her daughters to them.

Nine months ago she had convinced Zelophehad to try again for his heir. She was pregnant immediately and certain that this time God would give them the living son for whom they had prayed so diligently.

But Zelophehad had grown morose as the pregnancy advanced. Five months—six months—seven, and past the times when the male children had been miscarried. Eight months—he had not been able to bear the thought of another still little form—his would-be heir—being placed in the hole dug for him and covered with the soil of this awful wilderness—left for some wild animal to perhaps drag away.

Naronah talked and encouraged and was so very sure that this time he would hold in his arms a living son. But he finally had given up. Four days ago he had told Naronah he had to go and arrange for another wife.

She had cried and begged and promised. She had usually kept all mention of this matter from their daughters, but this time she groveled at his feet in the dust of the camp (for they were traveling as the pillar moved) pleading with him to wait until this child was born. She had cried, "You'll see how God has heard and answered!" She was almost screaming. "It is a man-child and he is alive and strong! Feel him moving! Please, please do not leave us—please wait and see."

He knew people encamped around them could hear their tragedy unfolding and that the men would think, *It's about time!* And that some of the women would laugh and say, "He has finally come to his senses."

He, himself, thought, *I've finally broken her spell. I'm going to find a young girl whose family has a strong history of producing male children and I'm going to have a son at last.* And this is what Zelophehad had told his almost hysterical wife so large with child. This is what his daughters and all the people camping around them heard him tell her.

"Naronah, I've known for a long time that it would finally come to this. You cannot give me sons! A man must have sons! I have been watching a family of Reubenites whose children are known to produce sons.

"I am going now to find and hire men to take care of the moving of our household and the herding of our animals. I am going to pay them to stay and help you and the girls, and I am going to find another wife and take her as soon as possible. I will have a son!"

And he had walked away never to see her alive again. *How could I have ever done this?* He knelt and kissed the cold cheek for the last time. "I could never love anyone as I love you," he said out loud.

Chapter 4

Zelophehad stepped outside his tent and looked toward the west. The sun was dropping low and the air was heavy with smoke. People around him were going about their evening tasks.

Women were cooking over fires built between the tents. The smell of manna filled the air. Some neighbors shared the fires; the women were laughing and visiting. Some preferred to cook alone.

Men were coming in from the edges of the camp after having settled the livestock and left one or two to keep watch overnight. Others were appearing from the interior of the camp where they had carried on business during the day.

Some of the older boys were carrying in wood and water and milk. Some smaller children were still playing around the tents waiting for the evening meal and their bedtime.

Zelophehad looked at the woman bent over the fire at the next tent tending something she was preparing for her family, and for a moment, he could see Naronah as she had tended their fire and prepared their meals all these years.

He noted again how far out of its place his tent was. He didn't recognize the neighbors on either side. His conscience smote him again for deserting his family at that critical moment. *I must have been mad,* he thought. *I was mad!* Then he spoke into the evening air, "I loved her more than anything in life, and now I've lost her."

Just then he caught sight of his four daughters coming from the outskirts of the camp. They were each carrying an earthen vessel—milk and water for the household. *They are good girls—beautiful children,* he thought. *Why do I treat them so badly?*

They approached slowly, their manner evidencing fatigue from physical labor and the wearing effect of their sorrow. He wanted to say something kind and comforting to them, but it wouldn't come out of his mouth. They didn't look at him as they passed.

Mahlah went into the tent first and set her water pot down. "Put the milk over by the back edge of the tent," she told the two younger. "I'll get out the manna that's left and we'll fix supper," Zelophehad heard her say. The girls were hungry, as well as tired, from working with the sheep.

All were trying to act as if their mother's body were not lying in the midst of them. "Hoglah, go out and set up some rocks so we can make a fire and . . ."

No need for that," Zelophehad interrupted as he stepped back into the tent. "We'll eat it cold and drink some milk tonight."

Yes, Father," Mahlah said, and motioned to Hoglah to bring the pot that held the manna that had been left from the morning gathering.

Hoglah just stood staring at the side of the tent. Zelophehad touched her shoulder and she violently recoiled. "Hoglah," her sister said, "bring the manna pot." This time Hoglah obeyed.

Mahlah was taking the clay bowls out of the woven reed box in which they traveled. She turned to Milcah and Tirzah, "Get your cups and one for Father, Hoglah, and me."

The girls dug into another box, handing out the cups. Mahlah set hers upon another of the reed boxes and handed out bowls after she ladled the ground manna into them.

Zelophehad watched and said nothing, although he had intended they not eat until after the burial in the morning. Hoglah poured milk into the cups and handed each a spoon. The little girls went to the side of the tent where they sat on rugs and ate in silence.

Their father ate standing. He finished quickly and set his dishes on the reed box by which Mahlah and Hoglah stood. All kept their backs to the still forms on the tent floor. When Hoglah finished eating he told her to take the younger girls and the jar of water outside and clean the dishes.

Hoglah helped the girls gather the dishes, picked up the water pot, and they left the tent. Mahlah looked at Zelophehad with a question in her eyes. He answered by asking, "Where is your mother's wedding veil? I know that she gave it to you long ago. I want to cover her and Oni with it before we put then in the ground."

Her heart broke as she heard his words. She treasured that beautiful veil more than anything she owned. She started to cry again. "But, Father, that would be the only thing I have left of her. Couldn't we use something else? We have a lot of beautiful linens. Please?"

"No, Mahlah, I want her to have it. Get it now for me and we'll wrap them in it before the girls come back."

Dutifully, she went to her own special reed box in which she kept her treasures and took out the pale blue veil. She could see her mother's face and the pride with which she had given the beautiful gift. "It is special," Naronah had told her. "It symbolizes our love and you are the first product of our love."

Tearfully and carefully Mahlah took it out of its safe hiding place and brought it to her father. It was like giving her mother up again.

Zelophehad didn't seem to care that it was so special. *I guess it isn't to him,* Mahlah decided.

The whole family rose early in the morning. Noah came in from keeping the sheep overnight and they all went out to quickly gather their manna. When that was done, Zelophehad instructed them to bring the wooden paddles every household kept. Then he lifted Naronah and their son and walked to the edge of the camp with the girls following.

There he selected a sandy spot and, with Hoglah's help, using the paddles, they dug out a shallow grave. Then he laid his only love and his only son, and they covered them with the sandy soil of the wilderness.

He knelt and told the girls to kneel and pray to Jehovah of the Israelites to gather their loved ones safely to their fathers, and the sorrowing girls did as they were told. Not one of them was crying. When they arose, he instructed them to bring rocks—the biggest rocks they could carry. There were rocks all around them—everywhere one looked. His daughters obeyed in silence.

He completely covered the grave with the rocks and set up a pillar of them—a pillar of remembrance—stacked all at the head of the grave. When this was finished, the girls stood with their heads bowed. They had arranged themselves in birth order, like stair steps. They were not weeping, but silently grieving and remembering. Their only source of nurture and love lay under this ugly pile of rocks.

Zelophehad expected at least one to say something—it seemed to him that they were always chattering—but no one spoke. They did not look at him; not one felt love any longer for this cold and stern man. He had lost them along with the wife and baby son—he was alone.

He waited a moment longer and then said, as he turned and started back toward the camp, "I must find where to get some of the red heifer water of purification and some hyssop. Tomorrow will be the third day since death defiled our tent. I must get some of the water and find a clean person to sprinkle us with it.

"I think I'll ask Joseph to do it for us since Hasenuah is also defiled; he probably has already located the nearest supply of the purifying ashes.

"Stay at the tent until I come and tell you what to do. We are all unclean until we are sprinkled tomorrow and again on the seventh day. He will have to sprinkle the tent and all the open vessels in it, too." He turned back to Mahlah. "Do you know where to find the other women who helped your mother?"

"Aunt Hasenuah will know, Father," Mahlah answered quietly. She was leading Tirzah by the hand, following him back to camp. Noah had an arm around Hoglah, guiding her along.

Milcah brought up the rear of their procession. She had always liked to watch and listen to her family. What a great void her mother's death had left. *It will be so sad without her; I don't think I can bear this sadness. I hate to leave her under those rocks.* Milcah stopped and looked back.

"Come along, Milcah. What are you doing?" her father called back to her. Then he said to Mahlah, "Do you know where we can find that man—the circumciser? He will have to be cleansed, too."

"Hasenuah will know, Father," Mahlah answered again.

Zelophehad led them to the tent and went off in search of Joseph.

Noah and Mahlah found stones and made a little enclosure for their cooking fire while Hoglah crushed the manna with mortar and pestle. The three worked together to mix it with milk and pat it into cakes to pan bake. They were so much later than their neighbors that some of them came out to see what was happening.

Mahlah tended the pans. Hoglah sat on the ground with arms around drawn-up knees, staring into the fire. Noah, who was usually very friendly and outgoing, did not want to talk to the women who appeared, but she saw her sisters were ignoring them so she spoke to them. She explained to all who inquired that her mother and baby brother had been killed and they had just buried them.

"We are all defiled and made unclean by the deaths, and so is our tent . . . " She motioned toward their tent which was much larger and richer than any of theirs. "My father is Zelophehad. He has gone to bring the water of purification and a clean person to sprinkle us and the tent."

The women were more than curious about this family which seemed to have but one male member. They had been observing all the comings and goings and how beautiful and interesting were these girls. They were delighted to find one of them so friendly and accommodating. They lingered a moment after Noah finished, but finding nothing else to talk about, they returned to their own tents.

Noah went back to Mahlah and helped remove the cakes from the pans as they finished baking. They smelled so good and she was very hungry, having missed her meal the night before. She picked up one of the cakes and started to eat. She loved the taste and the smell of manna.

Mahlah saw her take the cake and shook her head. "Noah, wait and we'll eat with the girls," she admonished her.

"I'm dying of hunger," Noah told her. "I haven't had a bite to eat since those cold cakes I had out with the sheep early yesterday morning!"

"I'm sorry, Noah. I forgot you didn't eat with us. There are so many things going around in my head." Mahlah looked as if she might start to cry again.

Noah finished the first cake and took another. "These are so delicious when they're hot. You are a very, very good cook, my dear sister!" she told Mahlah, hoping to evoke a smile.

"I had you and Hoglah to help, you know," Mahlah told her modestly, with just a hint of a smile.

"I know," Noah grinned and, piling the last bunch of little cakes on the platter, she headed for the tent with them.

Hoglah stood when Noah walked by her. She helped Mahlah throw dirt on the fire and they entered the tent to find Noah eating another cake and smiling down on the sight of two little girls sleeping in the corner with their arms wrapped around each other.

"Don't wake them, Mahlah," she said, as her sister started toward them. "That sleep will do them a lot more good than food at a time like this. God help them—and us!"

Hoglah found cups and poured milk for them and the three sat down to eat and wait for their father and for whatever life had in store for them now.

Chapter 5

After the purifying ceremony was performed that day and again four days later, things went back to normal in the household of Zelophehad—or, as normal as could be without the person around whom all the things that mattered to the girls had revolved.

Noah went back to the familiarity of life among the sheep and her caring cousin and friend, Asriel. He hurt when she hurt and tried everything he could to help brighten her days.

Zelophehad went searching and found the hired men who had deserted his family at such a crucial time. He dealt with them under the adjudication of the elder assigned to his family in the tribe of Manasseh when God told Moses to choose out seventy men to help him govern the people.

He did not receive much satisfaction, since that elder was discerning enough to see that he had deserted them first while the camp was on the move. But he did gain the small victory of having the wages he had paid them refunded.

Zelophehad had also searched through his possessions and found some of the jewels and Egyptian coins his father had taken as spoil at the time of the exodus were missing. It was a substantial, but not a grievous loss, to one as wealthy as he.

He surmised that the Amalekites had been frightened away before they could find his main treasure trove. He still was one of the wealthiest men in his part of the tribe and could well afford the help he needed to keep his family moving with the rest of the camp.

He spent two days away from his tent traveling to visit other relatives, searching for reliable servants. He found three. One was a young married man who would have to bring his own tent and his wife and two little sons to camp nearer Zelophehad. The others were two strong young men who still lived with a father who had many sons and few possessions. He agreed to furnish them a tent and also hire their sister to cook and keep house for them.

He would now have six hired men to help tend his livestock and help with the loading and unloading and setting up of the households as they moved. He would have Mahlah take over her mother's duties and pass her assistant's chores to Hoglah and Tirzah. He would keep Noah as a shepherdess and have her train Milcah on the job.

One morning soon after, when Zelophehad was out helping with the livestock, three men approached his tent and inquired of some women standing nearby if this was the tent of Zelophehad. The women told them that it was and stood by watching to see what was going to happen next to their interesting neighbors.

The men stood before the tent and hailed, "Ho! Zelophehad!"

Mahlah immediately stepped outside holding a manna pot. "Yes?"

The older man of the three asked, "Is Zelophehad at home?" He could not help smiling at the picture she made standing in the sunlight.

"No," she answered, "my father is out at the edge of the camp helping tend his animals, but if it is a matter of importance, I can send my sister to bring him." She was speaking to the older man but her eyes were on the tall young man standing beside him and smiling at her.

Obviously this was a man and two of his sons; there was a strong resemblance among them. She had never seen them before.

"Our business is of some importance," he told her politely. "If you don't mind, please send for him."

Mahlah turned and called inside the tent, "Hoglah, come outside, please."

Hoglah stepped out, and then took a step back with a look of alarm when she saw the strangers.

They all smiled again, thinking, *Here is another who will be just as pretty in a year or two.*

The older man saw the look of fear and hastened to reassure the girls. "I am Beerah. These are my sons, Hezron and Carmi. We are Reubenites. We are here to talk to your father about the wife he arranged for a few days ago," he said in a very gentle voice.

Now the look of alarm on Hoglah's face changed to sorrow and was mirrored on the face of her older sister.

"I see," Mahlah said in a flat tone. She turned and instructed Hoglah to go and tell their father that he had visitors.

Hoglah hurried away.

Turning back to the men, Mahlah asked, "Will you come in and wait? I will pour you some cool water or milk if you would like." She stepped back toward the tent door.

"That would be very nice," said the young man whose eyes had held hers for the long moment when she first came out of her tent.

"Please come in, and sit down."

She led the way into the large room and motioned toward an area with a beautiful rug; reed boxes evidently used as seats and low tables, and there were also piles of colorful pillows.

The room was cool and neat and had a particularly pleasant smell— manna and spices mixed with something they could not readily identify.

"Please sit and we will wash your feet," she offered and, as their eyes adjusted to the shade, they saw yet another beauty approaching with a basin and a towel. (This one was perhaps even prettier than either of the others.)

This one was a little one. She smiled into their faces and said, "I am Tirzah—my sister is Mahlah."

She knelt before the older man and Mahlah poured water into the basin and Tirzah expertly washed and dried his feet.

When she had finished, Mahlah put a cup of cool water into his hands.

What a pleasant place this is, he thought. *These girls are so lovely and accommodating, but there is something strange and different here.*

By the time Tirzah had performed the refreshing ritual on the third visitor and Mahlah was handing his cup to him, Zelophehad appeared at the tent door.

The three stood to greet him. Hoglah came into the tent behind him and the girls retreated to the far side making themselves as unobtrusive as possible while still near enough to serve if it was needed.

Zelophehad hesitated a moment until his eyes made the adjustment from the bright sunlight, then hurried to Beerah to embrace him. "Welcome to my home, Beerah!" he exclaimed.

The Reubenite returned the traditional embrace. "Zelophehad," he said as he stepped back.

His host interrupted by turning to the girls.

"Come and make these men welcome. Wash their feet and give them a cool drink," he ordered.

"Zelophehad, they have already done all to honor our visit," Beerah told him. "You have beautiful and gracious daughters!"

The man acted as if he had not heard the compliment.

Beerah could feel something unpleasant in the atmosphere and tried to ease the tension by turning to his sons.

25

He said, "Zelophehad, these are my sons. This is my oldest, Hezron, and my next is Carmi." He motioned them to come closer.

The young men stepped forward and embraced their frowning host as their father called each name.

"Please sit down," Zelophehad indicated the reed box seats and the pile of pillows. "I have been meaning to come and talk to you."

The men sat once again and settled themselves.

Zelophehad hesitated a moment and then he, too, sat down for the conversation he had been putting off for days.

"Sir," Beerah began, "did you not ask for my daughter, Metah, to be given to you in marriage as a second wife?" He saw Zelophehad's look of discomfort and could not imagine what was troubling this man. It had only been a few days since he had come to his home urgently seeking the agreement.

Beerah was getting the definite impression that Zelophehad would rather not talk about it now. But, it had to be talked about. Beerah's daughter was demanding that he do something to expedite the marriage now that the terms had all been settled.

"Were you not in a very great hurry when you came to us several days ago?" he asked the distracted man.

Now Zelophehad put out his hand as if asking for more time. "It is true, Beerah! But I did not know then what was happening at that very moment! My wife, Naronah, gave birth to a son and then the Amalekites stole into the camp and killed them."

The Reubenites were stunned. "You left your wife as she was having your son?" Beerah asked. "Did they catch the Amalekites? This is terrible."

Both young men had a look of horror on their faces. *No wonder this man is acting so strangely,* they decided.

"Yes, I left my lovely wife. I left her when she needed me most. I am ashamed of my behavior. It is a long and sad story. I loved my wife more than anything under the sun, but I can't change what has been done."

Zelophehad was not looking at his guests; he was staring at the door of the tent as if he expected someone to walk in.

Beerah sat looking at the Manassite with the handsome face. *What a strange man!* Zelophehad started to speak again. "I was at my wit's end when I came to you," he said so softly Beerah barely made out the words.

"Why have you not been back to tell us?"

Zelophehad was looking at him now. "We were all defiled by the deaths—our tent also. We had to be ceremonially cleansed with the purifying water—which took a week. Then I had to restructure my hired servant operation. I have no sons and have to hire help."

His voice was trailing off.

Beerah suspected Zelophehad was procrastinating because he hoped to be released from the marriage espousal.

"When will you be ready to take my daughter? We thought you were in a great hurry. She is expecting you right away."

Zelophehad nodded agreement. "I was in a hurry, but things have changed now and I was hoping to be released. Oh, I will pay the amount we agreed; I hope your daughter will not be offended. It's not that I find any fault with her—far from that! I think she would make a most desirable wife, but . . . ," again his voice trailed off.

"My friend," Beerah said, putting a hand on Zelophehad's shoulder, "I must stand for my daughter's rights in this. Metah is ever so pleased at the idea of your marriage. She will not take this lightly.

"If it were up to me alone, I'd release you—since I can see you now do not wish to take another wife and it would not be a happy situation. But, I will have to go and tell her that you are asking to be released. I guess the final decision will be up to her. She is strong-willed and she may want to take you before our member of The Seventy to force you to honor the agreement."

Zelophehad groaned inside. He did not wish to face that one again any time soon. The man made him feel like a worm.

"Please tell her I hold her in very high regard and that I do not want to offend, but I wish to be released, and I will still pay what was agreed. . . ."

Beerah's sons were standing by this time, seeing there was no point in further discussion. They walked toward the tent door.

Mahlah surprised herself by stepping toward the one who had held her eyes so long when they first saw each other. His father had called him Hezron, she remembered.

He smiled down at her, "Thank you for your kind hospitality." Mahlah felt a little catch in the vicinity of her heart and a kind of breathlessness—a very pleasant feeling she had never experienced before.

To her own amazement she reached out and touched his arm. "We were honored to have you in our home," she said, almost in a whisper.

He took her hand and pressed it in both of his own, smiling into her brightly shining eyes. "I'll come back," he said.

Behind them Hoglah looked at his brother and they both recognized what was happening between the smitten Hezron and Mahlah.

Beerah and Zelophehad walked by them and out the tent door. "Please assure your daughter that I wish her well," Zelophehad had started again.

"We'll see," Beerah said over his shoulder as he and his sons walked away.

Mahlah clasped her hands together, holding the knuckles of her thumbs against her lips and whirled on her tiptoes all the way across the tent and fell on the pile of pillows with a face all aglow with a new light.

Her sisters ran to her laughing out loud. They'd never seen her act so undignified. She laughed, too—never before so happy and thrilled.

Chapter 5

Noah woke with a start. *What was that?* She lay for a few minutes listening and wondering. Then she heard it again.

It was the blast of alarm the priests blew on the silver trumpets which signaled that God was moving the camp again.

She stepped to the door of the tent and out into the cold, calm morning air to see that the pillar of cloud had risen into the sky, ready to lead them in another move.

"It raised itself up while it was still fire, in the dark, early hours," Hoglah spoke from the side of the tent, where she sat, wrapped in one of their heavy covers.

"What on earth are you doing out here?" gasped Noah. "You really frightened me! How long have you been here?"

"I'm keeping watch," Hoglah said. "I've been here most of the night. I do this almost every night—it's hard for me to sleep."

Noah peered into her sister's face. "Hoglah, can't you tell me what is wrong? I know there's something really troubling you."

"I'm afraid, Noah, and I miss our mother. I just don't have anything to look forward to any more."

Noah put her arms around her. "Let me under your cover and we will talk."

Hoglah opened the cover for Noah to get in and then rewrapped it to hold them both snugly.

Noah said, "Let's sit."

They awkwardly managed to reach a sitting position.

Noah found her sister's hand and squeezed it. "Now, Hoglah, you do trust me, don't you?"

"Yes, I trust you, but if I tell you what I know, it might put you in danger, too. I wish I could talk with Mama and find out what I should do. I miss her so much, I'm miserable.

"Papa is so cold and hard, I'm afraid to even speak to him, let alone ask for help. What has happened to the Papa we once had, Noah?"

"I guess it was pride, and the long and constant pressure from everyone around him that changed him," Noah mused. "The same thing was working on Mama, you know. She knew she had to produce a son; and you see how it drug her down—trying to please Papa who was trying to live up to what his father and the rest of the people thought was his duty. I never will forget seeing our beautiful, proud Mama groveling in the dust, begging him not to go. He killed all the love and respect I ever had for him that day."

"What are you two doing out here?" Their father's voice came from the tent door. He stepped out to see the pillar of cloud raised high and ready to lead. "Get your manna pots and go gather for us. We need to eat and start taking down the tent. I want to have things ready before the blast sounds for us to move.

"I want our men and beasts to be ready to move up and retake our place in the order of march before the blast sounds for us to move.

"Get up!" he ordered the startled girls who were staring at him.

They rose and disentangled themselves from the cover.

"Do you think he heard?" Hoglah whispered.

"I don't care if he did," Noah flung back at her as they entered the tent to get the pots.

All the girls ran out to gather the day's food.

Zelophehad himself set out dishes for their breakfast to expedite things. He was determined to put himself, and his family, workers, and possessions back in their rightful place in the order of march.

After they had finished, he went to his livestock and directed the organization for the move. He had to show the new helpers where they should blend into the order once Ephraim, Manasseh, and Benjamin started to move out.

He brought back to the tent three of the young men with oxen and carts and donkeys to load their household furnishings and be ready to move.

The girls were already folding rugs, packing tent furnishings, and piling up the reed boxes ready for loading.

Levah, the young wife of Ishi, the newly hired servant, came hurrying up with his breakfast. "I took it to the place where you've been working," she told him, "but they said Zelophehad had brought you here." She handed him the large bowl and a spoon. His little son, Assir, stood holding his cup of milk. The other son, Jahath, was intrigued by all the activity and went climbing over the piles of furnishings to reach the animals.

"Catch him, Levah," Ishi warned his wife, "he may get trampled. We're in a great hurry and don't have time to watch for children."

Levah ran after the scrambling Jahath.

Ishi smiled down at his older son and took the cup to drink his milk. "You'll soon be old enough to help with the men's work, Assir," he said.

The boy beamed as his father drained and handed the cup back to him. "Right now, son, help your mother all you can to get our household packed and the tent taken down. I'll be back there with the donkeys as soon as we get the master Zelophehad's things all ready. Help your mother take care of Jahath; she has a lot to do since I can't help her right now."

Ishi hugged his wife who had caught the runaway and came back to him. "I'm sorry I can't help you more. I'll be there when I can. Hurry. Zelophehad wants us to catch up to his usual place in the camp, so we'll be leaving as soon as we can."

"Don't worry, Ishi," she assured him. "Assir and Jahath and I will have it all ready to load when you get there with the pack animals."

As she hurried off with the two boys, another young woman ran up to the tent. She also carried manna and utensils.

She stopped by Noah and Hoglah who were rolling up carpets in a well-coordinated routine. "Oh, can you tell me where to find my brothers? They were not where I usually take them their meals." Her hair was flying loose and her face was flushed.

"Don't worry, Ahitah, they are right over there helping my father," Noah pointed and then patted the girl on the shoulder. "Go ahead and take their food to them. My father can't refuse to give them time to eat," she said reassuringly.

Ahitah was grateful that her master's daughters were friendly and kind to her. Zelophehad treated her well also, what little he had to do with her, but there was something about his manner that frightened her a little.

She hurried to the place where her brothers were working.

Mahlah was inside the tent systematically pointing out what should be packed next. She had learned the routine from her mother and was teaching Milcah and Tirzah as they worked.

They carried things that did not go into the boxes out to Noah and Hoglah to be rolled or folded and tied and then loaded upon the donkeys when the men brought them. They placed beside each pile the rigging and ties and straps needed to secure the donkey load, and covers and straps for the ox carts.

Mahlah was standing in the middle of the almost empty tent deciding what to send out next time the girls returned, when a figure appeared at the door.

Her heart leapt. She instantly recognized Hezron. *Oh, how handsome he is,* she thought. She stood still and smiled and let him come to her. It made her happy just to look at him.

Hezron came near. He smiled, too, but she could see that he had something other than their mutual attraction on his mind.

"Hello," she said, warmly.

"I had forgotten just how beautiful you are, Mahlah. I thought I had kept my picture of you in my mind, but it doesn't live up to you at all."

She blushed, but kept looking into his face and told him truthfully, "I can close my eyes and see you any time I want. I cannot forget you." She was amazed at herself that she could say such things to him.

"How very sweet you are," he said. "You and your sisters have something about you that is difficult to . . . , I mean you are unlike the other girls I know." He felt stupid for not being able to express himself as he wanted.

Mahlah gave a little self-conscious laugh. "Indeed, we are different. We have a father who treats us as hired servants so we have no time or chance to learn how to charm and please men."

"Well, you certainly must have learned something somewhere, for you please me more than anyone I've ever met! I want to marry you if you'll agree."

Mahlah caught her breath and took a step back from him. At that moment, Milcah and Tirzah came back into the tent.

"What's next, Mahlah?" asked little Tirzah.

The spell was broken and Mahlah was pulled back into the real world.

"Take these boxes with our dishes and cooking vessels—in the order they are here," she pointed to each of three of the reed boxes. Make sure that this one is last; it has the things we will need as we make camp on the way.

"Then bring Noah and Hoglah and we'll start taking down the tent." The little ones hurried to obey.

Hezron looked at the slender girl and asked, "You even take down the tent? My sisters would faint if someone told them they had to do that." He laughed at the thought.

Mahlah didn't laugh. "We have no brothers. Father expects us to do whatever has to be done—and we do it."

"Oh, Mahlah, I would stay and help you if I could, but my father gave me orders to hurry back." He was embarrassed that he was going to walk away and leave her to that task.

Then Mahlah did laugh. "It is something that we do over and over. We are strong—all of us. But I think Tirzah is the strongest one of all," she added.

"Why did you come here today?" she asked, "in the midst of all the breaking of camp."

"My father was going to send someone to give your father a message and I asked to come so I could see you again."

Her heart began thumping again. *He has the strangest effect on me,* she thought. "What message could be so important that it would take you away from the moving preparations?

"I have instructions to deliver it and get right back." Hezron looked very serious. "My sister insists that Zelophehad honor the agreement that he made to take her to wife. If he does not, she is going to take him before the priest and judge."

To Hezron's surprise, Mahlah laughed. "Good for your sister!" she said. "Father is out helping with the donkeys and ox carts. You can go tell him now." She chuckled again.

She turned away and was looking for the two wooden mallets she always used to drive in or dislodge the tent pins from the ground.

Hezron was puzzled, but he had to hurry. "I'll be back, Mahlah, don't forget what I told you."

He was gone by the time Mahlah had located the mallets and turned around. "I wish we could have time to just sit down and talk to each other," she said quietly.

"I'll just bet you do!" Noah told her as the sisters came in. Mahlah sighed and handed the mallets to Noah and Hoglah, and they all went outside to begin the disassembling process.

By the time men came with the donkeys and ox carts used to carry Zelophehad's tent, the girls had pins, poles, ropes, leather straps, and both the fabric and goat hair coverings laid out and folded or rolled already to load in the reverse order to assembling.

Once again Mahlah supervised while the girls helped load. They finished quickly and the young men started toward their small tent to help their sister take it down. The trumpets sounded again.

"Come on, Hoglah," said Noah. "Let's go help Jahdiel, Eliel, and Ahitah." Time was getting short.

Hoglah looked toward the tent of Ishi where Levah was busy with the help of her son, Assir, trying to take down their small tent. "I think we'd better help Levah; she has her hands full, trying to work and to keep Jahath from running away."

She started toward Levah's tent where mother and son were trying to loosen the pins from the ground. She called back, "Mahlah, send Tirzah to watch that little boy and we'll help his mother and brother until Ishi gets here."

Noah followed Hoglah.

Mahlah nodded to Milcah and Tirzah. "Go help," she told them. "I'll stay here by our stuff. When you hear the next trumpet blast, get back here as quickly as you can."

Mahlah climbed up on the ox cart that she would be expected to drive in her mother's stead. She felt a stab of sorrow. *Everything reminds me of her.*

The loaded donkeys and the oxen hitched to their carts knew the routine and what was expected of them. They stood quietly in their places, waiting.

The smaller tents of Ishi and the brothers, Jahdiel and Eliel, came down quickly and the men arrived to help load. Soon Zelophehad's group was ready to move. He sent Noah and Milcah off to help drive the livestock and then he led the way through the Manasseh camp to his rightful place in the march once again.

His brother, Joseph, and his group were surprised to see them so early but glad to have them back close to family.

When that group finished their loading, there was even a little time to visit. Hasenuah and her two daughters came to talk with Mahlah, Hoglah, and Tirzah. The girls hadn't seen their cousins for weeks.

Everah and Lanodah had been born about a year apart after their brothers and they also had two younger brothers. Hasenuah had fulfilled and exceeded what was expected of a woman of Israel in the production of heirs. She was proud of herself on that account.

Everah and Lanodah were average-looking girls—not nearly as handsome as the daughters of Zelophehad. They were very amiable and pleasant company for their cousins whose lot in life left them little time for socializing and talking about things young girls usually enjoyed.

This day the talk centered on Miriam, the sister of their great leader, Moses. She had been looked up to among the Israelites as an example for all women.

"Did you ever see her in person, Mama?" asked Everah.

"No, I have to admit that I did not. But I have talked to people who did. They say she was a strong, intelligent, and kind person—and was very beautiful when she was young."

Hasenuah was looking, not at Everah but at her niece, Hoglah, as she answered the question. Hoglah was standing apart from the others, half hidden behind one of the ox carts—and would not look her aunt in the eye.

"What is the matter with you, Hoglah?" Hasenuah asked. "Are you ill?"

Hoglah shrank back at her question, then turned and walked back of Zelophehad's string of animals.

"Well, can you believe that?" Hasenuah asked Mahlah and the others. "Is she sick?"

"No, not physically sick," Mahlah answered. "She has been so strange since our mother and little brother were killed. I guess she just misses Mama and really feels the need of her more than the rest of us."

"Hmmmmm," mused Hasenuah. "I wonder if my talking with her might help. You know, talking to an older woman? Has your father tried to counsel her?"

Both Mahlah and Tirzah gave a little laugh at the suggestion that Zelophehad would actually try to comfort one of them. "No, Aunt Hasenuah," said Tirzah with surprising insight, "He's too busy feeling sorry for himself."

Mahlah reached and put her hand over the little one's mouth.

There came another blast from the silver trumpets ringing through the thousands of the camp of Israel. The men came hurrying toward them and the loaded donkeys and ox carts.

"I'll try to get to your camp tonight," Hasenuah told Mahlah and Tirzah as she turned to go mount her own cart. "I'd love to help Hoglah if I can. I miss my dear friend, Naronah, too."

Each Manassite took his position on his cart, driving or leading animals—whatever was needed—and they slowly began to move toward the standard of Ephraim.

That evening, after a long day's march following the pillar of cloud, all Israel halted when the cloud stood still, turning to fire as the light of day failed. The pillar stood still but remained high in the sky.

Zelophehad, his family, and his helpers made temporary camp and ate a supper of manna and water. As they were finishing their meal, Hasenuah walked into the circle of light made by their campfire.

"Greetings, brother," she said to Zelophehad, who sat on the ground leaning against his cart. "I came to talk with Hoglah if I may."

"With whom?" he asked.

"With Hoglah, if I may," she repeated, as Zelophehad stood and looked down at her.

"It's all right with me, sister," he said absently, and walked out of the light.

Hasenuah looked around and saw only Mahlah and Tirzah. "Where is Hoglah?" she asked in a quiet voice. "I'm all ready to try to help her. I've thought all day about what I should say to her."

The girls stared up into her face upon which the flickering shadows of their small campfire were dancing. "She's gone, Aunt, we haven't seen her since the last trumpet sounded. She's gone."

Chapter 6

Almost two months passed before the pillar that led them was halted and lowered. All Israel set up their tents in formation and once again settled into a daily routine. During the long days of travel Zelophehad had turned over and over in his mind the information Hezron had brought him the day they began this last march.

He realized that since he had made an agreement to marry Metah, the daughter of Hezron the Reubenite, he would have to go through with it or face the judge and the priest—unless he could convince her to release him.

As soon as his family was settled in, he told Mahlah that he was going to get the thing settled one way or another and walked away to the southeast toward the camp of Reuben's descendants.

He fervently hoped the girl, Metah, would be reasonable. Surely, if she realized she was unwanted, she would let him go. He no longer wanted a son. Naronah had given him a son and he had deserted them—left them alone to be killed by the Amalekites. He despised himself for that.

And Zelophehad's conscience was bothering him about the way he treated his daughters. They were beautiful and loving and obedient children. One could not ask for better children, but they were not boys.

He realized it was not their fault, yet when he looked at them he saw the tangible reason for all his trouble and sorrow. He didn't remember the happy times they had when the first three girls were small. He only remembered the shame and bitterness he felt when his father and brothers tried to convince him to take another wife. He remembered the way all the men looked at him and what he knew they were thinking each time Naronah's pregnancy produced a girl or ended with another tiny dead son.

It came to the point that when his two youngest girls were born he wanted nothing to do with them. When he had been called in to see the newborn, Milcah and the attending woman handed the baby to him saying, "It's another beautiful daughter," that he just looked into the tiny face and handed her back..

He shuddered now, remembering the stricken look on his Naronah's face as she had watched the exchange.

When Tirzah was born, he refused to even look at her.

Why did things have to end this way between me and my lovely Naronah? Was the God of Israel punishing us for loving each other more than we did Him?

The memory of his one love, his joy, his reason to live—the proud and beautiful Naronah—groveling in the dust at his feet begging him not to leave, tore at his soul. *Oh, if I had just waited one more day!* The thought rang over and over in his heart.

Zelophehad walked steadily away from Manasseh's camp under the tall brass standard of the ox of Ephraim toward the southeast, looking for Reuben's standard of the man. He had brought some manna to eat along the way on the first day, and he had a goatskin filled with water.

He walked through thousands of tents without really seeing any of the people. Often, he was greeted and returned the greeting automatically without recognition. He had left Manasseh and was well into the camp of the Benjamite tents when night fell. He found a space between tents among some rocks that looked like a likely spot. It really did not matter to him where he slept. He unrolled his extra garment—a cloak—which he had been carrying on his back, wrapped himself in it, and lay down to sleep among the rocks.

He dreamed all night about the same things he'd been thinking about in the day. He woke in the morning, gathered some fresh manna, and ate. He used some of his water to wet a cloth he carried and washed his face and continued toward the camp of Reuben and Beerah's daughter to face whatever that young woman had decided to do with him.

Zelophehad arrived at his destination late in the afternoon. Fortunately for him, Beerah's place was on the outer edge of Reuben and Reuben was next to Benjamin.

People he passed stared questioningly at this weary-looking stranger who stopped now and again to inquire after Beerah. He finally halted outside the tent he recognized from his previous visit. Several children—boys—were playing there. He asked one to go and tell Beerah that Zelophehad had come to talk with him.

The boy smiled and ran to the large tent and disappeared inside. Zelophehad watched the others scuffling, running and laughing, and thought, *What wonderful creatures little boys are.* His aching heart ached a little more at the sight of their merriment.

The little one returned and took Zelophehad's hand and led him to the tent, "Grandfather told me to bring you to him. You are welcome," he said.

As they came to the door, a young girl ran out and away.

Inside the tent Zelophehad's eyes adjusted and he saw a home much like his—maybe a little more decorated with pretty things—almost as rich.

Beerah rose to meet and embrace him. "Welcome, Zelophehad, welcome!" he said. "Take a seat, my friend. Take off your sandals. You have had quite a walk. My maidservant will be here to wash your feet in a moment, and I've sent for my wife and daughter who are visiting friends."

Zelophehad sat. He hadn't realized how tired he was. He loosed his sandals as a servant girl appeared in front of him with a water bowl and a towel. Another girl offered him water in a cup. He felt inclined to refuse it, but he was very thirsty. He took it and drained it. She offered more. "No, thank you," he said, trying to remain polite while he was feeling more and more defiant.

What a place to have put myself, he thought—*at the mercy of strangers—at the mercy of a slip of a girl less than half my age. What a fool I must appear to these people! What a fool I am!*

The girl finished washing his feet and he bound his sandals back on. *At least my feet feel better.* "Thank you," he told her, managing a smile.

The servant girl blushed and ducked her head. *What a handsome man Metah has hooked for herself,* she thought.

As the girl walked to the tent door, Beerah's wife and her daughter entered. Metah was a younger copy of her mother—average height, average looks. She was usually quite an agreeable person—a little pampered and spoiled by loving parents. But she thought this business with Zelophehad demanded firmness on her part.

She had decided that this poor man needed a firm hand to guide him into what would make him a happy life after all the troubles he had gone through with his first wife. When she saw him, she smiled, thinking how proud she would be to be called his wife. *He was still a young man and together they could easily produce an heir—or six heirs if he wanted!*

Her father motioned for them to sit. Zelophehad nodded to the mother, then turned his unhappy gaze upon her. "Zelophehad has come to settle our problem," Beerah told her and her mother.

"Will you be taking her back with you this time?" the older woman wanted to know.

Zelophehad stood and moved to where Metah was sitting. "I have come to beg you to release me," he said.

The girl opened her mouth to answer, but he put his hand up as if to ward off a blow. "Hear me out," he said. "When I came for you before, I was desperate to have a son—to fulfill my life's obligation and have an heir. I had born the shame of not having a son as long as I thought I could.

"But I found that shame was not half so hard to bear as the sorrow at the death of my wife, Naronah. She has been my life and my love since I was a little boy. It is my fault she is dead. I will never get over leaving her when she needed me most." His voice broke and he bowed his head.

"I can never be husband to another woman," he said. Then he was silent.

Beerah and his wife looked at each other, understanding clearly that their daughter would be making a terrible mistake to force this man into marriage.

"But I can give you sons. I can make you happy and you'll have a normal life—no more shame," Metah insisted.

"I don't want a son. I don't care about that any more. Naronah gave me a son. I don't want any other son."

Metah's mother took the girl's hand and looked into her eyes. "Give it up, daughter," she pleaded. "This will not make a happy life for you. There will be other young men who would be a good husband for you. Wait dear . . ."

Metah had been telling all of her friends how she was going to be the answer to this handsome and important man's troubles. She stood up and stamped her little foot. "I don't want another young man! I want to marry Zelophehad! If he refuses I will take him to be judged!"

"But daughter," began her father "can't you see how miserable this man is? You will not have a happy life."

Metah insisted, "I know I can change things for him." She faced Zelophehad, looking up into his sad and angry face, "I will marry you and we will have sons and you will be happy!"

"Daughter," Beerah tried once more.

"No," she said, "I am holding him to the agreement."

Her mother began to cry. "Is there no way we can change your mind, Metah?"

"No, Mother," she said, so calm and so sure she was right. She turned to her father. "The law says I have a right to make him take me as wife. I want you to start the proceedings now!"

"Very well," Zelophehad spoke suddenly, loudly, and looked into Metah's eyes. "I will marry you. I will live with you, but you will not be my wife. My wife is Naronah. Do you understand what I am saying?" He looked to the father and then to the mother. "Do you understand?" he asked the girl once more.

The mother drew in her breath sharply. Beerah put his arm around his shaking wife. But Metah lifted her chin and said, "We will have sons—many sons and be happy."

Thus, Metah became the second wife of Zelophehad, legally. He fulfilled all of the conditions to which he had sworn at the espousal. He went back to his place in the camp and prepared a place for Metah. He moved his daughters into a small tent of their own with all the old household goods and left the tent ready to receive her and the maidservant who came with her.

There was no celebration, as would later be developed as the custom in the land to which they journeyed, but Zelophehad went and brought her to this new (for her) home.

She brought with her elegant furnishings of which a household consist. The tent was soon very bright and beautiful on the inside. Zelophehad took no part in it. He came home to eat and to sleep and that was it. He was polite and kind to Metah, but somehow he always made her feel as if she were an intruder. The stubborn girl found she didn't know how to bring all her plans to fruition. She didn't know anything. She received exactly what he had promised. She had the title of wife of Zelophehad—the desire of her heart—but along with it, a leanness of her soul. She was far from happy.

Chapter 7

The two youngest daughters of the unhappy man, Zelophehad, had a relationship with each other that was far closer and deeper than with their older sisters, or that which the older sisters had with each other.

They had never experienced the happy family days before the lack of a son and heir rent the fabric of the home and family and left only the tattered relationship of Zelophehad and Naronah.

For as long as they could remember, their mother had been a grief-burdened person with the idea of having a son taking precedent over everything in her life. She was a good and kind and caring mother, but they could feel her deep sadness and it permeated their whole existence. Likewise they not only felt, but experienced, the growing bitterness and frustration of their father.

But they had each other and their common experiences, and they clung to each other and depended upon each other. They loved and admired their older sisters who were helpful and supportive, but it was to each other they looked for some sort of stability and emotional reinforcement in life.

When Zelophehad moved Milcah out to help with the sheep, it rocked them considerably. But when Hoglah disappeared he brought Milcah back to household duties once again.

Although it was a terrible loss and they missed Hoglah and were afraid of what might have happened to her, the end result was they were back together most of the time, learning to run a household under the tutelage of Mahlah.

With the coming of Zelophehad's new bride, things were even better with them. They did not have to endure the evident aversion of their father constantly, and they even had time to talk and play and daydream a little.

They worked together with Mahlah keeping their now, four-person household, and when Zelophehad needed them to help with the animals, he used them together as the equivalent of one herder or one shepherd. This made them even closer.

Their favorite entertainment was the after-supper stories Noah would tell them as they sat outside their tent under the starry sky. She would spin outrageous tales of adventure and sometimes intertwine tender love stories into the action.

Sometimes children from the tents nearby would sneak out and over to hear these stories and Noah would end up with quite an audience. They would never have admitted it, but some of the mothers caught onto what was happening and they, too, would steal away and come just close enough to hear.

The times that Milcah and Tirzah helped with the sheep or other livestock became times of enjoyment also because they would sing as they worked. Tirzah had a strong, beautiful singing voice and she used it frequently now that they had been separated from the immediate household of their father. She was not shy about singing for others. She sang the traditional songs—old as the family of Jacob—maybe older than Abraham. She sang the Song of Miriam, a song all of Israel's women knew. She sang when she was alone; she sang when there were people around. She sang. It was a comfort.

Milcah had a voice almost identical to that of Tirzah, but perhaps not so strong, and she was too shy to sing in front of people unless she sang along with Tirzah. Milcah's music was inside her—in her head—in her heart. She composed words to go with melodies that came to her. When this happened, she would hum the tune over and over to make sure she could keep it in her head. Then she would put words to it and teach it to Tirzah so they could retain it and be able to sing it together when they wanted. They had several of these songs—they called them Milcah's Songs.

Sometimes when Noah was near she sang with them, but mostly she listened while they worked. The men and boys who cared for nearby sheep and cattle enjoyed this background accompaniment to their chores. All of them knew who was providing it—the daughters of Zelophehad.

Chapter 8

Jacob and his sons had not entered into Egypt as fighting men—neither came they out as such, but most brought along weapons "borrowed" from Egyptians who were only too happy to see them go.

Israel was now into thirty years and more of wandering in the wilderness and they had learned a few lessons in warfare as the years passed by. Weapons and skill in the use of them were garnered along their way. Each tribe's men over twenty years of age made up its army. When they were needed, they were called—whatever number God deemed necessary.

There were days when the leaders of the fighting men of the different tribes would gather and go to the outside edge of the camp to practice their skills in warfare. They always brought their sons along to be trained, taking turns, so that the boys all received training, but that their regular duties were not left undone.

Asriel was among the trainees one bright morning when Milcah and Tirzah were called upon to fill his place minding Zelophehad's sheep. The girls were near enough so they could keep one eye on the sheep and the other on the war games.

The men used contests to practice their skills in races, and with bow and arrow, spear, javelin, dart, sling, and, rarely, the sword. The kind of battle that might be expected was mainly hand-to-hand combat, so that strength of arm and fleetness of foot were talents valued in the warrior.

Noah, Milcah, and Tirzah could not see the details in most of the contests, but some of the races were run close enough for them to see. They could hear the shouts of victory go up at regular intervals. They were hoping that Asriel would win in some of the competitions. All of them knew that he was very skilled with the sling—that would probably be where he excelled, but he was also very strong. They had not seen it, but he had told them he was getting good with the javelin and thought he might win some honors there and in the two kinds of wrestling they practiced.

Noah, also, carried a sling and pebbles to protect her sheep. She secretly wished she could be allowed to compete with the men slingers; she knew she was almost as accurate as Asriel, but did not have the strength for the distance he achieved.

Late in the evening the girls brought the sheep to the water. A sort of reservoir had formed at a low place with shallow areas to which the sheep could be driven and watered without having to draw water. They sat on the rocks to watch until their flock had time to drink their fill.

Some of the men from the war games came from upstream, passing on into the camp of the Manassites. The girls turned away from them and kept eyes on their charges. But soon they heard a familiar voice calling their names.

Asriel broke away from the men and came running to them. "Come," he said, "I want to show you off to some of my new friends and teachers." He stood with hands on hips, acting a little arrogant. Noah thought, *I think he's grown three inches taller since he left this morning.* But she said, "Asriel, you know we can't leave these sheep—beside, what do we have that we could show off?" She wanted to hear him say he was proud of her beauty.

"Noah, you know I think you are beautiful—and so are your sisters," Asriel told her. "I want the men to tell you who won the stone-slinging and came close to winning the javelin throw." From the way he was acting, the girls knew he meant he had won. They were all duly impressed, clapped their hands, and sent up a cheer of their own for their good friend and helper.

Two other men broke away from the group as they passed. Milcah looked at them and decided they were brothers, but on second look, changed her assessment. One of them had to be the father. The other might be a little older than Asriel and Noah. They were not of the tribe of Manasseh as far as she could tell; they had a slightly different appearance. She noted that each carried a javelin, as well as a sling, and each had a scrip fastened to his girdle in which to carry the stones for the sling.

"Girls, this is my teacher, Abdon, and this is his son, Malcham. They are Benjamites and very good warriors," Asriel announced.

Noah found she was strangely interested in Malcham. She could see the admiration in his face as she smiled and gave her hand to his father, then to him. She reached out and drew her sisters to them. "We are pleased to meet you," she said. "I am Noah and these are Milcah and Tirzah." The girls dutifully gave their little hands to greet the men politely.

Admiration was nothing new to Noah; she was so accustomed to it that she actually expected it when she met a man. She knew for sure of the three young men whose families had already asked for her to be given to them in marriage. Her father had firmly rejected each offer. And there were most likely others she knew nothing about. She really didn't care; she had no wish to marry any one. It surprised her that these thoughts had popped into her head as she looked at Malcham.

Abdon was asking her little sisters for a drink of their water. They ran happily away to bring their goatskin canteen. When they returned Tirzah handed him a cup and Milcah poured water for him and then for Malcham. There was something different about the way these men received the cup.

"Oh, you're both left-handed," Noah exclaimed.

Malcham smiled at her as he gave the cup back to her little sister. "It's nothing unusual among us Benjamites," he said. "In fact, it is unusual if you are not left-handed."

Asriel didn't like the way his new friend and Noah were looking at each other. "Tell the girls about the sling contest," he reminded Abdon.

The older man nodded and said, "Asriel is the best slinger of all the men in the competition we held—both in accuracy and in distance!"

Noah stepped closer to Asriel and gave him a hug. "We just knew that some of that cheering we heard was for you!" Then she grinned as she saw him grow another couple of inches in height before her eyes, and she teased him, "But I can still beat you!"

Asriel laughed and told the men, "She can't, but she surely comes close." Then he looked at Abdon, waiting for him to tell the other news.

Abdon nodded again. "This is the first time Asriel has entered the javelin throw competition—and he finished second to Malcham!"

The girls clapped their hands and cheered again and Tirzah announced to the visitors, "We are not a bit surprised." This brought a laugh from them all and Tirzah was pleased to join in.

The sheep seemed to have finished drinking from the water pool and were beginning to wander away in all directions. Milcah and Tirzah picked up their staves and started after them, one to the right and the other to the left of the water.

Abdon watched them gather the flock and start it toward the common area to spend the night with neighboring flocks. "Those two actually know what they are doing!" he told Asriel.

"Of course they do. Noah and I trained them well."

"But they are so young . . ," began Abdon.

Noah interrupted, "They will have no time to be young and carefree. My father thinks of us as servants and we do whatever work comes to hand. Haven't you heard of Zelophehad of Manasseh? He has no sons!"

Asriel heard the unfamiliar bitterness in her voice again.

"Zelophehad?" asked Malcham. "Father, isn't that the leader we were told to talk with?"

Abdon nodded. "Yes, we were to consult with him as head of one of the families we worked with in the training games." He turned to Asriel. "He wasn't out there today, was he, Asriel? He is your uncle, isn't he?"

Asriel shook his head, "Yes, he's my uncle, but I don't know where he was today. I wish he could have seen me compete. My father and other uncles said I'm a credit to our family." Asriel had experienced a very satisfying day.

Noah looked at the lowering sun. It was getting late. She reluctantly told Malcham, "I'm sorry, but I have to go help Milcah and Tirzah." She started away. Malcham walked after her. "Will you be coming into camp?"

"No, since Asriel will be taking part in the celebration, the girls and I will have the night watch of the sheep in his place." She hurried along. Malcham kept pace.

"But I can't let you go like this! I just found you. I will come back this evening after we see your father! Where will you be?"

"Near the common sheep area," she called back laughing, as she started to run toward her flock.

Malcham stood looking after her a second and then walked slowly back toward Asriel and his father.

Chapter 9

There was a celebration in the camp that night of the warriors of the tribe of Manasseh. Some of the swiftest runners had chased and killed four roebucks. The game had been roasted over a campfire and eaten along with the evening manna as a special treat after the games. Abdon and other instructors in different skills were introduced and thanked.

Young men who had won contests were presented to all attending—their names called for all to hear and honor and remember. After this, several leaders spoke exhorting all Manasseh to be strong and brave for whatever might be in store in the wilderness and when they entered the land God had said would be theirs.

Asriel took Abdon and Malcham to introduce them to Zelophehad who had not attended the games or the celebration. Asriel left them at Zelophehad's tent after introducing them. Zelophehad invited them to come in and sit with him.

Abdon delivered the greetings from the leaders of the tribe of Benjamin and also an invitation to attend their war games the next time they were held. He noted the presence of this man's very young wife, but Zelophehad did not call her forth to meet his visitors since they had already been welcomed and dined with the other men of war.

Zelophehad was not rude but certainly not cordial. He accepted the greetings and spoke the right words for his answers, but Abdon received the impression that the man's heart was not in it and that he would be glad when they left.

Searching for something to fill the lapses in conversation, Abdon remembered how impressed he had been with this man's daughters.

"We met your young daughters after the games today," he said.

"Yes," answered Zelophehad.

Abdon was smiling remembering the pleasant time he had with them. "You surely must be proud of such beautiful and gracious girls."

Zelophehad's expression did not change. "Yes, I am."

"I was especially impressed with the way the two little ones handle the sheep," Abdon ventured. Surely this would evoke some acknowledgment from a father's heart. But it didn't. Zelophehad did not even smile.

"I think they have learned well."

"And Malcham here is quite taken with your Noah," Abdon said, smiling at the remembrance of his oldest son's immediate attraction to the beautiful shepherdess. As far as he knew, this was the first time Malcham had shown interest in any girl.

This finally brought a reaction. Zelophehad looked straight at Malcham. "She has already been asked for over and over. She is too attractive for her own good. She is spoiled and vain."

Those were the most words he had spoken since they had arrived. Both visitors were taken aback. They sat silent for a minute and Abdon got to his feet and said, "We must be keeping you from your rest. We'll be going now so we can get an early start back to our camp in the morning."

Malcham and Zelophehad both stood. Zelophehad said, "Thank you for your expert instruction of our young men. Tell your leaders that I will probably attend your games next time. I have had some difficulties, but things should be back to normal by that time."

He gave the required embrace to each, in turn, and led the way to the tent door. "Good evening," he said as they started to walk toward the campfires.

"I believe that is the strangest man I've ever met," said Malcham when they had walked away. "He certainly doesn't know his daughters, does he?"

"No, he doesn't," agreed the father. "It's as if he has no feelings at all—just an empty heart." I feel so sorry for those little girls. They are so anxious to please. I don't see how a father could be so indifferent.

"He said he had had some difficulties, but what on earth could turn a man to stone like that?"

By this time they had reached the campfires where all the men of war and their trainees were still celebrating. Someone was telling a war story.

"Dad," Malcham put a hand on his father's shoulder, "I told Noah I was coming back tonight to see her."

Abdon smiled. He remembered the feelings of excitement that Malcham was experiencing. "Yes, I heard you."

Where are you—we—going to stay tonight?"

"We'll just find a spot inside the camp and roll up in our cloaks for the night," he said.

"But, I need to know where to meet you," Malcham told him.

"I'll just come along and visit with the little ones while you and Noah talk and get to know each other."

"That's awfully good of you, Dad. Those little girls will be thrilled at the attention."

"But I know I'll enjoy their company as much as they enjoy mine," Abdon said, and meant it.

They stopped and asked directions to where the flocks were kept together at night. It turned out to be about a half mile away. They walked in silence. They were not tired and looking forward to the visit.

They reached the flocks—all bunched together in the middle with the shepherds at their campfires at intervals on the perimeter. The night was clear and still and lighted by the moon and stars. It seemed like an enchanted night to Malcham—he loved it. Just the faintest hint of a cool, gentle breeze touched his cheek now and then. He thought, *Why have I never noticed how wonderful the night is?*

They stopped at one fire. "Can you tell us where Zelophehad's flock is?" Malcham asked the man who had risen from his place by the fire with his rod at the ready in his hand.

"Who are you?" he asked. These shepherds rarely received night visitors.

"Please—we are friends! I am Malcham and this is my father, Abdon. We are Benjamites here for the games. My father is one of the visiting instructors."

"Oh," said the relieved shepherd. He had heard of Abdon. "I am glad you are not intruders! Zelophehad's girls are about five more campfires around our circle. Just follow the music and you will find them."

They thanked the man and continued around the circle. Neither of them had noticed the music before, but now it floated to them on the gentle breeze, fragile and lovely as the night itself.

"Isn't that beautiful?" asked the astounded Abdon of his son. "What a melody! I don't think I ever heard that before, have you?"

"No, Father," Malcham answered in a very soft voice. "It sounds so sad it makes you want to cry," he admitted. "I can't make out the words; I'll bet they are sad, too." The nearer they came to the source, the more the singing touched their hearts. It ended just as they reached the girls' fire.

All three girls jumped to their feet with their rods in hand. "Who are you?" Noah asked. The men stopped. "It is Malcham and Abdon," the father called out. "May we come in?"

The girls relaxed, laughing in relief.

Malcham walked to Noah saying, "I am sorry we frightened you." He put his hand on her shoulder and felt she was trembling.

She pulled away with an embarrassed little laugh. "One always has to be ready out here. I'm not afraid for myself, but I worry for my little sisters." She walked to where Abdon stood. "We are pleased to have your company again."

The little ones hugged him. "Yes, we are very pleased," echoed Tirzah. Milcah's brightly shining eyes let him know she, too, was happy to see him again.

"Was that you doing the beautiful singing we heard?' he asked, looking down at their upturned, delighted faces. They both nodded enthusiastically, noting the stress he had put on the word beautiful.

"Will you sing some more for me while Malcham and your sister talk and get to know each other?" He was laughing and they were giggling as they agreed.

Malcham led Noah away from the fire and Abdon sat down and patted the ground on either side of him. "All right," he said, "I'm ready and eager to hear more."

The girls were beaming. "Let's sing him Naronah's Song," said Tirzah. She started without waiting for Milcah to agree, but Milcah joined in on the third note. It absolutely thrilled Abdon's soul. Tears welled up in his eyes.

Beautiful and lovely Mother,
Tender and caring Mother,
Can you see us, your daughters?
Where are you now?
We need you. We miss you.
Where are you now? Where are you now?

The last notes of the melody died away. Abdon swallowed the lump in his throat. "Oh, that is so wonderful, girls. Who taught you that song? But it sounds so sad. Who is Naronah?"

Tirzah answered, "Milcah made up the song. Naronah is our mother."

Abdon swallowed hard again. He reached out and pulled the fragile body on either side against him in a firm, tender embrace. *How could Zelophehad be so indifferent these precious, helpless children?*

He kept his arms around them and they leaned against him. "Milcah," he said, "you have a wonderful gift from our God to be able to make songs like that."

"I know it is a gift because it just comes to me," she answered. It was so easy to talk to this kind man—something rare for her. "It just comes into my head when I least expect it, and I sing it over and over so I can teach it to Tirzah. She's a much better singer than I."

Abdon was intrigued. "How many songs do you have?"

You mean of my own? We know a lot of old songs, too. Our mother and sisters taught us. We can sing Miriam's Song."

"Not the old ones, "Abdon persisted. "I'm asking about your own songs."

There was silence for a moment while they tried to decide how many. Finally Milcah said, "We don't know how many, but there are a lot of them. Sometimes they are happy like the one I made about the hart."

"Does your father ever ask you to sing for him?"

"No," said Milcah, "it upsets him."

"Upsets him?"

"Yes," Tirzah elaborated. "Once, after our mother was killed, I saw he was so sad and I wanted to help him. I got Milcah and we asked him if we could sing our song about the hart for him. Milcah didn't want to, but I thought it might help him. It's really a happy song." Her voice quavered and trailed off.

Milcah took over. "Father looked up and nodded his head so we began to sing. Then he just got up and walked out of the tent. We never tried again. But we sing all we want while we're out here," she finished happily.

"How about singing another one for me?" Abdon asked.

"We'll sing all night for you," Tirzah told him.

"If we sing too far into the night," Milcah chuckled, "the other shepherds might start throwing rocks at us."

"It is getting late," their visitor agreed, "but sing me one more before I have to tell Malcham we must go."

Milcah leaned around Abdon and said, "Let's sing the Eagle Song for him. It's my very favorite."

"Eagle Song, you say? That sounds good."

"Yes," Tirzah agreed, "that's one of the best ones. I love to watch the eagles in the sky." She began to sing and, again Milcah joined on the third note.

> Brave and worthy eagle—you rule the sky.
> Come and take me to your home in the highest rocks.
> I want to live the way you live.
> Cover me with your strong wings—take care of me,
> Watch over me.
> I would come to you now if I could fly,
> If I could fly.

It made Abdon's heart pound in answer to the wild longing in the words and the minor key melody. He sat silent.

Tirzah looked up at him. "Didn't you like that one?" She was disappointed.

"Like it?" he cried, "I think it is absolutely wonderful! I wish I could take you home with me to meet my family and sing for them. I know that they would love it, too."

"I wish I could be in your family," Milcah told him. "Could you marry me when I get old enough?" She was shocked to hear herself utter these words; she was usually so shy. But she knew she might never see him again and he was so kind. And she thought he was very handsome—even more than her father. Somehow, it was easy to ask the question there in the dimming and flickering campfire light.

Tirzah didn't move or say a word. She knew Milcah was saying what was in her heart. After a moment Abdon spoke. "I'd be proud to have a wife like you—so beautiful and talented, and such a good worker. Anyone would be proud. I'm flattered that you think that way about me. But, as you said, Milcah, you are too young now. We'll wait and see if you still feel that way about me in a few years."

Abdon was deeply touched by the openness and vulnerability of this strange and exceptional child. He hoped his answer let her know he valued her esteem.

He gave them both another hug and rose to his feet. "It is time for us to go now."

"Malcham," he called in a little louder voice to the pair who had been sitting just outside the circle of firelight.

Noah and Malcham appeared immediately in response to his call. They looked so happy and sad at the same time. "I wish we didn't have to go," said the younger man.

"I feel the same way son. But we must. Abdon took Tirzah's hand, then Milcah's, and then Noah's. "I am honored and grateful to have been allowed to know you daughters of Zelophehad," he said.

Milcah's eyes were shining with tears. Abdon felt like crying, too. He turned away to Malcham, waiting for him to say his goodbye.

Malcham followed his father's lead, taking each girl's hand. But he leaned forward as he held Noah's hand and kissed her softly on the cheek. "I'll come back," he said.

Then the men disappeared from the light of the campfire. Tirzah went to Milcah and put her arms around her. Noah stood still a minute, staring into the dark after the visitors. She put her hand to the cheek Malcham had kissed. Then she took her rod and scattered the coals of the dying fire. She picked up some dirt and threw it on the coals. The girls sat down together to wait out another night in the wilderness.

Chapter 10

Iloriah, the wife of Beerah the Reubenite, had never quite recovered from watching her oldest daughter willfully and stubbornly force the man Zelophehad to keep his agreement to marry her after he had openly told her she was not wanted and that she would be his wife in name only.

Metah insisted she knew what was best and would not listen to older and wiser counsel. Iloriah realized that she and Beerah had been spoiling their daughters by giving them anything and everything they wanted, without teaching them responsibility and respect for others.

When Beerah and Hezron had come back from visiting Zelophehad's home that first time with such praise for the man's daughters, she had felt some twinges of guilt. And when Metah put on the performance of forcing the man to marry her against his will, Iloriah realized she had failed with her daughters.

They had done very well with their sons, but their daughters were a different matter. She knew there was nothing she could do now to change Metah, that her oldest girl was probably learning some bitter lessons. So, Iloriah vowed to try to teach Sharvah, her younger daughter, to be a responsible person who could think of something beside her own desires in life.

Part of this, she knew, was simply learning to work. Iloriah had worked before she became Beerah's wife. She had helped her mother with all the chores that went with running a household with Israel on the move.

Even after she had married, it pleased her to continue some of those chores, but Beerah was a wealthy man and head of one of the most prominent families in the tribe of Reuben. Gradually, she had turned more and more of the work over to the servants.

Beerah seemed to think that all she and the girls should do was keep themselves looking as attractive as possible and live the good life that God had given them. He enjoyed spoiling the three of them with nothing to do but eat, sleep, and visit and entertain friends.

But after his visit with the daughters of Zelophehad he could not stop lauding those girls for how they worked. Iloriah had to admit that she was a little hurt and jealous and thought he was comparing them to her and her daughters.

This particular morning she had dug out her loom and was preparing to give Sharvah a lesson in weaving. She reasoned that would be a start without being too much of a jump from complete inactivity. She had purchased plenty of yarn from the spinners—black yarn of goat's hair. They would start with the most practical weaving—tent covering.

Iloriah was quite pleased with her idea. She had sent her two youngest sons off to work with their father and brothers this morning. The boys were eight and ten and ready to learn all about raising and caring for livestock.

The weather was so pleasant that she intended to set up the loom outside the tent and let Sharvah ask some of her friends to come and see the demonstration, too.

Hezron came walking around the side of the tent and was surprised to see his mother surveying the result of all her work in setting up the loom and making ready to start weaving.

"Mother! What are you doing out at this time of day?"

"It might surprise you to know that I'm going to do something useful for a change," she replied cheerfully.

He came to her and kissed her on the cheek. "I didn't know you were a weaver," he said looking at the loom and the big basket of yarn. He really was surprised.

"You don't know a lot of things about me. I have grown old and lazy and I intend to do something about it!" She was so proud of her firstborn, and she wanted his approval as well as that of Beerah. "I may not remember it all at once, but I used to be very skillful at it."

She could see that he did approve. "I am going to try to teach Sharvah and some of her friends."

Hezron grinned and shook his head. "May the Lord be with you then—dealing with that group," he said jokingly.

Iloriah dropped he basket of yarn she was moving and turned to her son. "Are they that bad, Hezron? Have we really let it get that bad?"

Hezron saw the concern in his mother's face; she was almost in tears. "Oh Mother, I didn't mean to upset you." He came and hugged her. "It's not all your fault."

"But it is, son—mine and your father's. We have seen to you and your brothers' training for a useful life, but we have been so blind about the girls. Look what has happened to Metah! I am so worried about her, and it all came about because she is so proud and selfish."

"I have been thinking about going to see her," Hezron told his mother. Then he added, "I want to ask for Zelophehad's oldest daughter to be my wife."

That made his mother smile. "I've been expecting that. I have never heard such a glowing report as you and your father brought back about those girls!" Then her smile faded. "Son, are you sure you want to deal with that poor man? I hate to see another of my children drawn into that unhappiness." She was looking earnestly into his eyes.

"Yes, Mother, I have considered that. But I really admire and care for Mahlah. She would make a wonderful wife. I know you will love her and she will love you."

Iloriah wasn't so sure having a daughter-in-law like Hezron and Beerah described would be all that great. She'd feel as if she were being compared all the time—and falling short. She told her son, "You know your father and I want what is right for you and will make you happy. Have you talked to him about it?"

"Oh yes, Father thinks Mahlah is wonderful, and Zelophehad is a wealthy man, you know."

"But what does your father say about dealing with him again? He will be the one who has to bargain with him."

Hezron hesitated, then answered, "He said I'd better go and talk to Mahlah first, then if she is agreeable, ask Zelophehad if he'll consider it. We've heard that several have asked for Mahlah's sister, Noah, and that he will not allow her to marry."

Iloriah hugged her son. "I guess you'd better go, then. If this is what you want, I hope he says yes, but he is such a strange man. I guess he has had enough to make him strange, though."

Hezron looked at his mother and thought she must be the best mother in all Israel—and the most understanding. "I plan to leave this morning. Do you have anything you'd like to send to Metah?"

Iloriah shook her head. "No son," she said. "I think that is the problem. We've given her everything she wanted until she thinks she's entitled. She is probably learning a bitter lesson now . . . Just tell her we miss her and love her."

Hezron started to walk away.

"Son, take care of yourself," she called after him. "I love you and am so proud of you!"

He came back and kissed her 'bye again. Then he walked away and soon disappeared among the tents.

Hezron's journey into Manasseh's division of the camp was a long and boring trek, but he cheered himself with thoughts of the girl he had decided to marry. He thought he saw the hand of Jehovah God in the way they met and the instant communication and understanding they had experienced.

After all the young women and girls he had known and not found himself attracted, suddenly and unexpectedly, he had found this one, Mahlah, and knew instantly she was the one to marry.

He sensed she felt the same way about him. But to be sure he had to make this visit and they had to find time to really talk and get to know each other.

He made a mental list of what he knew about her. She was beautiful; of course, that was the first thing he had seen. She was also gracious and appeared to have been schooled in the fundamentals of hospitality. She was very agreeable and seemed to get along with all those around her. This he could tell by the way she treated and was treated by her little sisters. Her father was very wealthy and a respected leader in the tribe of Manasseh.

Those were all pluses, but he had to admit there was something on the minus side. If he married her, Zelophehad would be his father-in-law and that might bring a lot of trouble with it.

Hezron and his father had talked about this. Zelophehad's attitude toward his daughters might very well carry over into the relationship with the son-in-law. Hezron knew he could not be as tolerant of Zelophehad's disdain as were the girls, but then he wouldn't be around him that much if he took Mahlah with his own tribe.

Also, there was the relationship, or the lack thereof between his sister Metah and Zelophehad. That silly girl had put herself in an impossible position. God only knew what would happen there. Maybe Metah would swallow her pride and ask for a bill of divorcement. They all knew that the man would readily agree.

Chapter 11

When Hezron reached the small new tent Zelophehad had acquired to house the girls, he heard someone singing. He called out to Mahlah and she appeared at the door holding some sort of garment she was evidently working on.

Her eyes widened and brightened with pleasure when she saw him. "Come in! Oh come in, Hezron! I am so happy to see you again." She reached out a hand and pulled him into the tent. Inside, Milah and Tirzah stepped forward to greet him and then went to get the welcoming drink of water and the bowl and towel with which to wash his weary feet.

He stopped them saying, "Girls, thank you, but let's delay the amenities a little while. I have to talk to Mahlah about important things and have little time. I also have to visit my sister Metah while I am here."

They stopped in their tracks and waited. Hezron had to smile at the agreeable picture the three made looking expectantly to him. He spoke to Mahlah, "Is there some place where we can go and talk? Somewhere we would be alone, but still where people can see us?"

Tirzah offered, "You could go where we water the sheep. That's a nice place and it also has some little trees for shade." She was smiling up into Hezron's face.

Mahlah said, "It will mean a little more walking for you, but it would be ideal. We would be out in the open, but we could keep to ourselves. Are you up to another mile or so?" She was looking to him in anticipation.

He reached for her hand. "We can talk as we go."

Mahlah hesitated a moment and told the girls, "You two can stay in the tent. Run to Levah if you have any problem. I'll be back in a little while."

They nodded their assent. They were laughing because they could see how happy Mahlah was to have Hezron back with her, and they could read the look of pleasure on his face as he and Mahlah walked away.

"I have come to make sure that you will marry me," Hezron said, squeezing her hand. "I have to find out how you feel and then, if you agree, I have to arrange it with your father."

Mahlah answered, "Yes, oh yes, Hezron. I think that is what I have wanted since I first saw you." She laughed self-consciously. I was surprised at the way I acted toward you. I had never done such a thing before in my whole life. Something just made me talk to you. Then I was afraid of what you would think of me!"

"I thought you were wonderful—and so did my father."

"Hezron, you must consider many things before you make up your mind."

"I know, and I have been thinking of nothing else since the last time I saw you. But one thing is sure, I've never before felt the way I do about you. I think God brought us together."

He let go of her hand and put his arm around her shoulders. She leaned against him and nestled her head against his shoulder as they continued to walk.

They found the watering place and found a rock to sit upon under one of the scrubby trees.

They talked and talked about everything they could think of—getting to know things about each other. How precious the time. How happy their hearts for this little bit of time together. How sad having to think of ever having to part.

But that had to be considered. They discussed all the pluses and minuses Hezron had come up with and tried to think positively about whether Zelophehad would let his daughter go. Mahlah had very strong doubts.

Hezron was keeping watch of the shadows and the position of the sun. Their time was slipping away. Finally, he had to tell her, "We must go back. I have to go see Metah and I will ask your father when he comes home."

Mahlah sighed. "I wish we didn't have to go. But come back with me to our tent and we'll get you a drink of water and something to eat. You must be hungry."

"I hadn't even thought of food," he said as they stood, preparing to go back. Mahlah took two steps and stopped, and turned to face him. "There is something we haven't discussed, Hezron, and I know firsthand how important it is. We must talk about it or our marriage could be doomed from the very beginning." She was looking straight into his eyes and tears were welling up in hers.

"What is it dear Mahlah? Of course we must talk about something that important. Tell me . . . ."

"It is what happened to the two people that loved each other more than any two I've ever heard of—my mother and father! Oh, Hezron, what if I am not able to give you a son?"

He stepped back from her. With all the thinking and planning he had done, that thought had never occurred to him. "Mahlah, that is important, even if we do not want to think about it now, we have to."

"Yes, we have to agree what we will do if that should be true," she said. "I know I am the one who has to say it, Hezron. If I can't have sons you will have to take another wife before it has time to make us bitter. It makes me so sad even to think about it, but we will have to act before it has time to twist us and hurt us and ruin our lives as it did to my parents."

She held out her hand to him again. He took it and kissed it. "I agree, Mahlah. Thank you my dearest girl. I pray we will never have to talk about this again."

After Hezron and Mahlah returned to the tent, she prepared manna for him to eat while Milcah and Tirzah gave him water and washed his feet.

The youngest girl chattered happily to him as he ate. Milcah smiled approvingly upon him each time she caught his eye. They both liked him and were happy for Mahlah to have someone who loved and cared for her. They had guessed he was going to ask their father for her tonight.

Mahlah sat quietly watching Hezron and the girls. Her heart pounded when she thought of him asking her father to let her marry him. *Would this be the last time she would ever see him?* Tears ran down her face; she could not keep from crying.

Hezron ate quickly. He could hardly wait to speak to Zelophehad. He had no fear of the man—only the knowledge that this strange person could control his destiny.

He saw Mahlah's tears. "Mahlah, this manna tastes wonderful! I've never had it prepared this way. You are a good cook!"

She wiped her eyes. "There are many ways to prepare it. God gave us something wonderful in manna."

"Mahlah is the best cook in the camp," Milcah assured him. "She may be even better than our mother was."

"Another plus for you, Mahlah."

She managed to smile at him. He stood, wiping his mouth on the napkin they had given him, then laying it by his dish on the reed basket table, he said, "Well, I must go on to Metah's."

He thanked the little girls for their hospitality. Then he turned to Mahlah and held out his arms. She came to him and he kissed her. It was so sweet, it thrilled their souls. It was a promise of what might be to come or of what never would be. He turned and walked out of the tent. Mahlah sank down to the carpet, weeping quietly.

Hezron walked quickly to Zelophehad's tent. It was late afternoon and men were beginning to return from business and work. Women were preparing their fires to begin cooking the evening meal. Children were still running free, but closer to home as they saw the women tending fires.

Several people spoke to the tall young stranger. He returned the greetings without really seeing them.

He stopped outside the large, impressive tent and called, "Metah! It's your brother, Hezron!" He waited several seconds and was about to call again when someone appeared at the tent door.

"I'm looking for Metah"—he started, and then realized this was his sister. She had aged ten years in the few months she had been away from home. Gone was her

imperious manner. She was not unkempt, but he could see that she no longer tried to keep up with the latest look in dress and hairstyle. In a word, he was shocked at the change.

He came closer to her, "Oh little sister, has this Zelophehad been beating you or mistreating you?" She gave him a sisterly hug.

"Hezron, it is so good to see you." She laughed. "No, Zelophehad hasn't laid a hand on me. He literally has not touched me—as he promised.

"I have learned a lot in the last few months. It has been a difficult lesson—humbling. But come in and visit. Westrah and I will make you welcome. My husband probably will not be here for another hour or so. He always waits as long as he can before he comes home at night." She led the way back into the big tent.

Hezron could see how she had decorated and adorned the tent. It was very welcoming and attractive. "You don't need to go through the greeting ritual," he told her. I have been at Mahlah's tent. They gave me food and drink."

"They are really sweet girls aren't they, Hezron? They have treated me well. What did you have to see them about?"

"I came to see if Mahlah would marry me. And then to ask Zelophehad for her to be my wife."

Metah was greatly surprised; she had known nothing about their relationship. If someone had told her, she probably had been too preoccupied with self to have really heard.

"You and Mahlah! Oh, I think that would be fine, Hezron. She will be a wonderful wife." Then she stopped smiling and her face took on a troubled look. "You know that he has refused at least four different offers for Noah, don't you?"

"I don't know that much about any of it. I have heard rumors. I only know I love Mahlah and she loves me. I have to ask for her!"

Metah patted him on the shoulder. "Maybe he will let her go. He keeps Noah to tend the sheep, but now since I and my maid are here to keep his house, maybe he will let Mahlah go.

"But. Hezron, I have to warn you. This is a very unhappy family. Weigh the consequences well before you make an affiliation to it."

Hezron received her warning with a sympathetic ear. *She really has changed,* he told himself.

Westrah, the maid, came toward the front of the tent on her way to get the fire started for evening meal preparation. Hezron greeted her with a friendly smile. "Hello, Westrah, how are you? I must say we have missed you."

"I am well, Hezron. And we have certainly missed you and your family and your happy home. It is quite different here," she said as she went on out the door.

Metah led Hezon to the sitting area of the tent. "We may as well sit and talk," she told him. "Tell me all about our mother and father and good old Carmi and the children." She motioned for him to sit on a pile of beautifully colored cushions and she sat opposite him to listen. "I have missed all of you so much!"

He began to tell her what he could think of that had happened since she left—wondering at the change in her. She was interested in the least little detail. They were both so involved in the conversation they did not see Zelophehad enter. Suddenly he was standing over them.

"Well," he said, "so we have family visitors!"

Metah stood to acknowledge his presence and went to bring water to him. Hezron stood and was greeted with the usual embrace exchanged by men. "Greetings brother," said Zelophehad, and motioned him to sit again.

But Hezron was in a hurry to get to the business at hand. He looked upon the handsome face of his brother-in-law whose eyes constantly expressed a sadness along with anger. "Zelophehad, I have come to ask you if you will allow your daughter to marry me," Hezron blurted it out. *No use in senseless skirting around the issue.*

"No! No! No!" Zelophehad cried in a loud voice. It was not just his eyes that were angry now; he was angry all over. "How many times must I tell you young men that I will not let that vain and selfish girl marry? No! Noah cannot marry you!"

Hezron was stunned by this outburst but tried to maintain his composure. "But sir," he began.

"No! I said no!" Zelophehad slammed a fist down on one of the reed boxes, sending ornaments and dishes flying.

Metah and Hezron stared at him in unbelief.

"But," Hezron tried again and when Zelophehad began to shout, Hezron shouted louder, "I am not asking for Noah! I am asking for Mahlah! Surely you can't call her vain and selfish."

Zelophehad calmed himself. "Mahlah is it? Mahlah, you say? Why would you want to marry Mahlah?"

"Your daughter is beautiful and good and a hard worker. I love her and she loves me. She would make anyone a wonderful wife."

"I guess you expect a great dowry, since you know I am wealthy?" Zelophehad asked."

"I want her if you offer no dowry at all, and I can pay whatever you ask. I am also wealthy," the frustrated young man answered.

Metah put her hand to her mouth. *That was a mistake; Hezron isn't doing so well in the bargaining,* she thought.

Zelophehad smiled, surprising the two young people. "The answer is, no. I will not talk about it further. She cannot marry you, or anyone else. I warn you not to try to see her again. Now, leave my tent," he ordered.

Hezron looked as if Zelophehad had struck him. He knew there was no use in arguing. He turned to go.

Metah screamed at her husband. "You! You are not human! What reason could you possibly have to keep these two apart? Is it to get revenge against me?" She started to cry. She reached out to Hezron. "Wait, brother, I am going with you."

Metah turned back to the smiling Zelophehad. "I want a bill of divorcement. You can list whatever you like as the reason."

Zelophehad's eyes and his smile registered triumph. "Gladly," he said. "You shall have it as soon as I can get it written! And I'll send along all this stuff you've scattered in my tent. Now, you may get out, too," he said calmly. "Go!" he repeated, pointing to the door.

As the young people came out, Westrah was waiting with a look of shock on her face. "Metah, I have to go, too. Let me get a cloak for each of us. It will be cold outside tonight."

Metah was still crying, but nodded consent. Hezron reached out to stop Westrah. "Do you want me to go in with you? There's no telling what he may do!"

"No, Hezron. He won't hurt me; his anger is all toward Metah," she said in a voice that convinced him she would come to no harm.

As they stood waiting, Hezron put an arm around his distraught sister. "Don't cry, Metah. It is not your fault. I believe he will not let any of his girls marry. God help them! Oh, my poor, sweet Mahlah!"

At that moment, a slight figure slipped out of the darkness and ran straight into his arms. "I'm so sorry, Hezron," Mahlah cried. "I'll love you as long as I live!" She held him and kissed him again. Then she thrust his cloak and skin water bottle into his hands and disappeared among the tents.

Chapter 12

Zelophehad was mightily pleased at winning his freedom from Metah. That silly girl had been sure she knew what was best and right for him. She wanted to change him and to run his life.

For months it had pleased him to wear her down with no other weapon than complete indifference. As she had held the nuptial agreement over his head and thought to force him to do her will, so he had held indifference over her. His had proved to be the more powerful weapon.

To a self-centered and selfish girl accustomed to being pampered by loving parents, indifference had been a destructive force. Then when Hezron came to ask her husband for Mahlah, and Zelophehad had treated him with such disdain, it had been a crowning blow to her self-esteem. Then all she wanted was to be as far removed from the man as possible.

The very next day, Zelophehad went to the judge and to the priest and then to the scribe for consultations about the bill of divorcement and to have it signed, sealed and ready for delivery to Metah along with all the possessions she had left behind.

He wanted all vestiges of her presence removed from his tent.

The judge and the priest had told him that he must list something about her that didn't please him. "That is not difficult," he told the scribe when he had the bill written. "Just write that she is selfish and she is a nag. Nothing I did pleased her and nothing she did pleased me. The marriage should never have been in the first place!"

The scribe shook his head and wrote as Zelophehad instructed.

Next day Zelophehad went to his daughters' tent and told them they were to come home and resume the routine they had "before Metah."

"I want you to come and pack everything that belonged to that girl to be sent to her father's house along with the bill of divorcement as soon as possible.

I will send Jahdiel and Ediel with the donkeys and Ahitah with an ox cart if necessary, but I want all of her things out of my way!"

This was not good news to the girls; they would be losing their freedom from his disapproving presence. Mahlah was heartbroken at his treatment of Hezron and refusal to allow her marriage. It was difficult for her to even look at her father.

The younger girls had long ago given up on any expectation of love or consideration from him. But the move back meant less time to just forget their situation and enjoy their little occasions of time together and with their sisters.

It was less of a change to Noah, who spent very little time away from the sheep. It was no surprise to her; she knew her father had never forgiven her for her outburst at him in front of the women at the time of her mother's death.

She had heard the words he had used against her over and over in his refusals. Noah asked the God of Israel to help her to show people that she was not the girl he described her to be. She didn't believe she was selfish. She suspected she might be a little vain about her beauty, but not enough to hurt people. She liked people.

Noah did not care that her father had refused the young men who had wanted her as a wife. She had never wanted to marry. She was sorry he was treating Mahlah this way. Mahlah had never disobeyed Zelophehad and had always shown him respect. Beside that, Mahlah and Hezron were in love and Hezron was considered a very desirable match. There was no reason that Noah could see for Zelophehad to refuse.

It hurt Noah to see Mahlah change from a glowing young girl, full of love and hope, into the sad creature who had given up on happiness and was set on just getting on through each day.

Also it meant there was now absolutely no hope for Noah, herself, to ever have a family as long as her father lived. Meeting and getting to know the young Benjamite, Malcham, had stirred strange feelings in her soul. She had guessed it must be love because she had never felt such tenderness toward anyone. These feelings had caused her to dare a faint hope for happiness—that her father might someday change his mind and forgive her and allow her to marry. But with this treatment of the obedient older sister, her hopes vanished.

Her father was a completely different man from the laughing, caring father of her childhood. It was difficult now to even bring up such memories in her consciousness, so she seldom tried.

Noah looked at her little sisters and thought how sad their lives had been. *Poor things*, she thought. Yet, they struggled along and managed to find some joy in each other and their music and her stories. They had experienced nothing with which to compare their miserable existence. *What is ever to become of us?* she pondered.

Within a few days the girls had scoured Zelophehad's tent, removing all of Metah's finery—all the colorful clothes, furnishings, and decorations that their young stepmother had so enthusiastically brought into her marriage. They carefully packed it all and loaded three donkeys and an ox cart for the hired men and their sister to take to the Reubenite camp.

"Take it to Beerah's tent, unload it as he instructs, be polite and follow his orders and then return as quickly as possible," Zelophehad told the three, who were secretly pleased to be getting away for a while.

As Jahdiel and Eliel led off with the heavily laden donkeys and Ahitah climbed upon the ox cart and it slowly lumbered away, visitors arrived at Zelophehad's door.

Joseph and his wife, Hasenuah, had not visited his brother in over a year, but they showed up on this day, of all days, bringing their daughters along to visit their cousins.

Zelophehad and Joseph had business to talk and went for a walk to inspect sheep and other livestock. Milcah and Tirzah were most happy to see the agreeable Lanodah and Everah once again. These daughters of Joseph were older than they and were looked up to for that reason, among others.

But this day the little shepherdesses had to leave to help Noah so Asriel could fill in for the hired men Zelophehad sent to the Reubenite camp. They hugged their aunt and cousins and talked a few minutes with the visitors before Zelophehad's impatient looks toward them caused them to hurry away to join Noah.

This left Mahlah to entertain the cousins and their mother. She graciously brought them into her father's tent and gave them cool water to drink. The girls giggled as Mahlah performed the foot washing ritual on each of them and their mother. It seemed strange to them that their cousin, whose father owned this impressive tent, was doing the work of a servant.

Besides, they had never before had their feet washed in this manner. They seldom left home. They looked down upon the shining hair of Mahlah as she worked and squirmed and giggled self-consciously.

When Mahlah began on Hasenuah, the aunt neither squirmed nor giggled. Her thoughts were that all the possessions of this girl's father might have been hers if he had not refused marriage to her long ago. As Hasenuah watched the sad and beautiful girl washing her feet, the thought came to her that the daughters of Zelophehad could not inherit the land which God had promised to be parceled out once they entered the land of Canaan. Should something happen to Zelophehad, the girls would not inherit this land.

Their father would not permit them to marry. This meant there would be no grandsons as well as no sons.

If there were no Zelophehad, no sons or grandsons, the double portion of that land which should go to the oldest would pass on to the next oldest, which was her husband, Joseph. She smiled at the thought. They would be rich, indeed.

Mahlah had finished her task and was standing in front of her. "Are you hungry, Aunt?" she asked. Hasenuah heard her but was reluctant to give up the daydream she was enjoying. "No dear," she said, "we have been eating all day. We had some manna snacks on the way over."

"All right then," Mahlah said, "we can have some time to just sit and talk." She enjoyed visiting with Hasenuah and her girls. Her aunt had always been kind to her, especially, she thought, since the death of her mother. What Mahlah actually wanted now was to run away somewhere and cry, but she knew it was her duty to entertain these visitors.

She sat beside Everah and smiled at Lanodah and Hasenuah. She could not think of anything to start a conversation.

The aunt had no such problem. "Have you ever heard anything from Hoglah?" she asked.

Mahlah was surprised. She had been expecting a question about her father's refusal of Hezron. She shook her head. "We've heard not one word, Aunt. I wonder if my sister is dead. It has been over a year, now."

"I wonder what could have happened to her," Everah put in. "People don't just disappear—or do they?" She turned to her mother.

"No, they don't," Hasenuah told them. "There has to be a reason or someone with a purpose behind it."

"But who could have a reason or a purpose to take one ordinary eleven-year old Israelite girl? Surely someone saw her. It is really a little frightening—it might happen to any of us. I have prayed that she is all right," said Lanodah.

Mahlah nodded. "We, I mean the girls and I, pray for her every day. Father never mentions her."

"Your mother's death has deeply affected him," Hasenuah said, leaning over to pat Mahlah on the shoulder, "but then I guess you realize that more than any of us."

"He has become very cruel," Mahlah agreed quietly."

Then came the conversation she had expected.

"I was very sorry to hear Zelophehad refused a very generous and desirable offer of marriage for you," Hasenuah said.

Mahlah tried to make her expression as indifferent as possible. "I should never have allowed myself to even hope for happiness—then I should not have been disappointed. I just should have known better. He blames us, his daughters, for all his problems," she said in a flat tone.

Everah and Lanodah had heard all about how Mahlah and Hezron had been so in love and how their uncle Zelophehad had quashed it with a few words. Now they could see Mahlah's grief and tears began to roll down their cheeks.

Their open show of sympathy touched Mahlah. "Don't cry for me dear cousins. Don't let our unhappy home reach out and affect you, too. Be thankful you have a mother and father who love you and will care for your future."

Turning to Hasenuah, she expressed the hopelessness she had been feeling since the night Zelophehad had driven her love away. "Aunt, I don't know what will ever become of us. I guess we will live and die with no purpose if our father will not allow us to marry and have children."

Mahlah had already wept so much that she seemed to have no tears left. She just stood in front of these sympathetic three with drooping shoulders and bowed head.

Hasenuah got to her feet and wrapped her arms around the despairing girl. "Mahlah, you could very well have been my daughter. Remember, Joseph and I will always be ready to help you and your sisters if you need us.

"There is nothing we can do with the situation like it is now, but when your father dies and the land that will be allotted to him in Canaan passes to Joseph, you do not have to worry. We will take care of you as our own!"

Mahlah thanked her aunt. "That is very good of you." But, something in Hasenuah's tone of voice caused her to stiffen, and Hasenuah's evident confidence that one day she and Joseph would be in control of what actually belonged to her and her sisters struck a warning note in Mahlah's consciousness.

Chapter 13

Hoglah was not dead. She was making a much happier life for herself than she would have had if she had not run away.

She thanked the God of Israel every day for the kind people to which He had led her. She realized what a dangerous thing she had done and that she could very well have fallen into wicked and cruel hands. But she had feared for her life and had been compelled to remove herself as far from harm's way as possible.

She did not know if the killer had seen her, but she had certainly seen the heartless murder of her helpless infant brother. And she knew in her heart if one could thrust an arrow into the body of a newborn babe so sweet and innocent, that one was also quite capable of killing an eleven-year old witness to silence her.

It had been Hoglah's idea to move into the center of Israel's camp—near the priests and Levites. She somehow reasoned she'd be safer there. While the whole camp had been waiting for the "forward march" that day, Hoglah had taken a bottle of water from one of the donkey's riggings and a cover from the ox cart Mahlah was to drive, and started walking away from Manasseh and the killer.

There was endless activity as each family prepared to begin the march, and no one had paid any attention to an eleven-year old girl walking in their midst. When the trumpet had sounded to move, she had just kept up her pace in the direction they were headed. Then she had tried to move a little faster than the others so she would not be close to any group for any length of time.

She did not have to carry food—only a small pot in which to gather her manna. She was not conspicuous gathering it because everyone else was gathering their supply before the sun could ruin it.

Hoglah savored the taste of manna. The girls had been taught many ways to prepare it for variety, but she liked it just as well raw—or in the form it was found on the ground—as most of the other ways. On this trek she would gather and sit close enough to one group of travelers as to appear unto others she belonged to them, but far enough away that the people would not think she was encroaching.

The pillar of fire sometimes led them far into the darkness of night; it did not automatically halt at sundown. When it finally halted, the travelers also halted. Sometimes they made campfires; sometimes they just unrolled beds and went to sleep.

Hoglah discovered a great way to sleep comfortably and also be hidden. She would move around as the campers were settling in, find an ox cart and watch to see that the owner did not remove anything from it for the night. Then, when the owners were settled for the night, she would climb in with her cover and sleep securely.

The pillar had kept Israel on the move for over two weeks that particular time. Hoglah's method served her well until she had reached the section past the Kohathites—the sons of Levi who carried the disassembled sanctuary and she figured she was past the center of the camp. She was now in the section which consisted of the tribes of Reuben, Simeon, and Gad, under the standard of Reuben—the standard of the man.

It had been bound to happen. She overslept one morning and woke to see faces all around the cart, peering in at the young intruder.

One of the faces belonged to a sturdy, near middle-age woman who called out to someone not far away, "Reuben, come and see what he Lord has dropped into our cart!"

Hoglah lay still, staring back at all these people, frightened so badly she was trembling all over.

Reuben came and peered down at her, too. "By the great Pharaoh's long, black beard!" he said. "Anthah, I believe the Lord has finally answered your prayers and sent you a girl—and a pretty one, at that!"

Reuben was a man of about forty years with twinkling eyes and a happy countenance.

Hoglah could see that the six other faces staring at her were of boys ranging in age from about eight years up to fifteen—and they had all started to laugh. She forgot her fear and sat up. "What are you laughing at?" she demanded indignantly, scowling at them. This brought on more laughter, but the younger boys backed away from the cart.

Their mother put out a gentle hand to Hoglah who had begun to tremble again. She had hidden her face in her hands but did not cry. She had promised herself long ago that no matter what happened, she wouldn't allow herself to cry.

The laughter died away. They could see her terror and were ashamed they had laughed. Anthah held up her arms and told Hoglah, "Come on down, dear. We won't hurt you."

Hoglah could hear the kindness in her voice. She allowed Anthah and Reuben, who had stepped up, to take her hands and help her down from the cart. They both felt the violent trembling. As she stood in the midst of this family of Reubenites, she suddenly felt safer than she had in along time. "I'm sorry I slept in your cart without asking you," she told Reuben, "but it seemed safer than sleeping out in the open."

"Indeed it was," he agreed.

"Who are you, dear?" Anthah asked. "Where did you come from?"

Hoglah saw no point in lying to them. If they tried to make her go back she would run away again. "I am Hoglah, she said. "My father is Zelophehad, a leader, a wealthy man in the tribe of Manasseh."

To Hoglah's surprise, Reuben laughed again. "I'm sorry, but I can't believe you."

"And why not?" Hoglah tried to stand taller. She looked him in the eye and then to Anthah's face. *Neither of them believes me!* she thought.

"Would the daughter of a wealthy man have such rough and work-worn little hands?" he asked.

Hoglah was dumbstruck. She looked from Reuben to Anthah. "And would she be dressed as you are and so dark from working in the sun?" Anthah added. "Forget we asked you. You can tell us when you are ready," she said in a sweet and kind voice and smiled at Hoglah.

In the meantime, come and help us gather manna and we'll all have breakfast together." She took Hoglah's hand and turned to her six sons.

"Here are my dear boys," she told her. "They are my life's work," she added proudly. "Hoglah, this is Hanoch," Anthah began, indicating the tallest. He grinned at Hoglah and she could not keep from grinning back at him.

"Then this is Pallu; and this is Azaz; and this is Joel; and this is Shemaiah; and this is my youngest, Gog," Anthah said, pointing to each in turn. They each looked sheepish and grinned as his name was called.

What a family! Hoglah thought, *I like them all!* "I'm sorry I yelled at you," she told them. "I was awfully scared! I've been scared for a long time." Reuben and Anthah exchanged understanding looks.

"That's all right," said Gog. "We yell at each other all the time." The others all agreed, still grinning.

"Come, come!" said the father. "We must gather our food and be ready to move!"

The boys would have loved to stay and talk to this pretty young girl, who, evidently their parents were prepared to take in—and find out why she had run away and where she had come from. But they knew they must gather the day's manna before time to move—or they would go without food all that day. All ran for their manna pots.

Hoglah went back to the cart, reached in, and brought out her own small pot which lay beside her water bag and covering. She looked at Anthah, who smiled and held out her hand again, saying, "Come and help me, Hoglah."

Thus, Hoglah was taken in by this happy Reubenite family with no more questions asked. She fell easily into their daily routine. Anthah had been given the daughter for whom she had long waited. It was as if her place in the family had been waiting for her. Hoglah had been given another mother—a much happier, if not so beautiful mother.

And how thankful Hoglah was for this new father. Reuben was strong and hard working. He was a good-natured Israelite who was, by all accounts, a happy man. Instead of four unhappy sisters she had these happy-go-lucky brothers. Things could not possibly have been more different. The boys loved to tease her and play practical jokes on her. They had never been close to a girl before and they delighted in her presence in the household.

There was often laughter in Reuben's tent and Hoglah found herself laughing as much as any of them and teasing the boys as much as they teased her. It seemed some happiness had found her at last.

But when night came and she lay trying to sleep, she sometimes woke herself crying out, and sometimes Anthah would wake her telling her she was safe in their home and no one could harm her,

She still remembered that awful scene and she prayed to the God of Israel to help her resolve what she should do about the thing she had witnessed.

Chapter 14

Malcham, the son of Abdon of the tribe Benjamin had not forgotten Noah, the daughter of Zelophehad of the tribe of Manasseh. The short time he had spent with her had spoiled him for any other girl of any tribe.

He thought about her constantly and talked with his father about her several times. Abdon admired her almost as much as Malcham, but when his son talked with him about the possibility of a marriage, the man was obliged to bring up the subject of dealing with Zelophehad.

"Malcham," he cautioned, "that is a very unpleasant situation. The man who would be your father-in-law seems determined to make his daughters' lives miserable. I don't believe he would allow Noah to marry you, or anyone.

"But supposing he did agree—have you considered how his animosity would affect your lives? The girls are barely handling it themselves. Think how it would wear on you, you who have a normal relationship with your mother and me. I know that you would feel obligated to respect him as you do your parents and older relatives, and I can't see how that would be possible considering only his actions.

"There is no telling what he has done that we know nothing about, but at the least, would you not want to protect Noah from his malice and resentment if she became your wife?"

Malcham had to admit he would be very angry with someone who would try to hurt the lovely Noah, who seemed so harmless and agreeable to him.

"But Father," he said, "we would not be around Zelophehad and his family if we were to marry. I would prepare a place for Noah here, among my loved ones, in my father's house. You would want us here, wouldn't you? You don't think Noah would be a bad influence, do you?" That question entered his head while he was speaking.

"Oh no, Malcham!" Abdon assured him. "I think she'd probably be a good influence, but son, you've only talked with her twice. These troubles she's been through might have affected her in some way we cannot see on casual short visits with her." Now that the idea had been voiced, he had to consider it might be so.

"Malcham, that part of it would have to be between you and Noah; it would be none of my business. What I am concerned about is the man, Zelophehad, and what he might do to you and your life. I have to tell you I think there is something very wrong with him, and it pains me to think of your becoming involved with a dangerous man."

Abdon put his arm around Malcham's shoulders as they walked and gave him a hug. It hurt him to see this dear young one, who was so optimistic by nature, worrying about the troubles caused by one so obviously selfish as Zelophehad.

It would certainly have surprised him to know that the strange, unhappy man had once been very much like Malcham.

"Father, our war games will be coming up very soon," Malcham said.

"Yes, I think it's only a month or two," Abdon agreed.

"Zelophehad said he'd be coming to the games."

"He did tell us that, didn't he?"

"Father, I think I will ask him for Noah at that time," Malcham said.

Abdon's heart skipped a beat. He had so hoped Malcham would decide to give up on Noah. "Malcham," he asked, "are you sure there is no other girl for you? I've heard your mother talking to you about others who have shown interest—others who would not bring along a whole set of problems into marriage."

"There is no one else, Father. I have no interest in marrying unless it is to Noah." Malcham's mind was made up.

"You know," reminded Abdon, "that Zelophehad has refused several offers for Noah's hand?"

"Yes, I know, but she wasn't in love with those men. She told me that she wasn't even interested in marrying when they asked."

"And you think she'll be interested if you ask? You think it will make a difference with her father?"

"Father, I think she loves me and would marry me if I asked."

Abdon pursued the question. "Are you sure? Did she tell you that?"

"No, I'm not sure. She didn't tell me in so many words." Malcham was trying to remember every word of the conversation they had that one night. The feelings they had were so new to both of them that trying to put them into words, or just expecting them to be understood all seemed to blend together in his memory.

Abdon understood. He was not so old that he had forgotten such feelings. "Son, you are going to have to go back to see Noah and get this settled for certain before you think any more about asking her."

"I know you are right, Father. That's what I'll have to do and I want to do it before the war games." It seemed Malcham had made up his mind about this also.

"I'm thinking about starting tomorrow if you can spare me. I love you, Father, and I don't want to make you unhappy, but I really want to go." Malcham had stopped and was looking into Abdon's eyes.

Abdon told him, "It isn't a matter of my happiness about your marriage: it is a matter of your happiness for the rest of your life. If you feel you must go—go!"

Malcham left early next morning for the camp of Manasseh. His young heart was full of anticipation of seeing Noah again. Somehow he knew that this special girl who had so many admirers—and who never seriously considered another man—had found him special, too."

But when he would think of all the men who had admired her—and at least four who had asked for her—he would begin to doubt such a prize as she could actually care for him. Then he would carefully go back over the talk they had that night outside the light of her shepherd's campfire.

Every thing she had told him led him to believe that she felt differently toward him than she had toward any other man, and she was as surprised at her feelings as he was at his. He certainly knew he was unskilled at matters of the heart, but Noah had no reason to deceive him. He suspected she was unskilled also. She had talked openly and frankly about caring nothing for marriage with those who had asked for her.

But she had expressed fears that her father might never allow her to marry. Such a situation would be a tragedy for any woman of Israel, whose reason to exist is to give her husband an heir and to bring forth sons and daughters of Abraham to make Israel a great nation.

Happy indeed would be such a woman whose marriage also included love of the man for the woman and the woman for the man. Malcham knew of marriages all around him made for convenience' sake. He, of course, did not know the inside details of how the matches worked out, but the people seemed to get along all right and did not appear to be particularly unhappy.

But, why settle for that when you could have that, plus the joy of love to crown the union? No, he did not wish to settle for just an ordinary existence, waiting for the appearance of an heir to fill up his life.

Malcham reached Manasseh's camp in the early morning of the third day of his journey. He was familiar with the way they handled their sheep and other livestock and had no difficulty finding Zelophehad's flock and herd.

The sheep were peacefully grazing on the grass and plants the Lord always seemed to provide at the places where the pillar of fire stopped and lowered. *Peace, grass, and water for the animals—peace, manna, and water for the people,* was the thought that came to Malcham's mind as he looked at flocks as far as the eye could see.

As he walked toward Zelophehad's flock, he saw two figures sitting on rocks facing their charges. It was Noah and Asriel. Malcham felt a twinge of jealousy toward his friend, Asriel. *Why should he get to spend so much time with Noah?* he caught himself thinking.

As he drew closer he saw Noah slide off the rock seat and stare toward him. *I believe she has already recognized me!* It gave him a happy little thrill. *She does care for me!* he assured himself. He quickened his pace and the girl began to run toward him. Something made him stop and open his arms. Noah ran right into them.

"Oh Malcham, I think I love you!" she greeted the happy traveler.

He folded her in his arms and they remained that way a long moment. Then he held her away at arm's length and looked into the beautiful dark brown eyes he had not been able to forget. He said, "I finally figured out that I'm in love with you. I don't know all that much about love, but I think that must be what's wrong with me. I have thought about you every minute, waking and sleeping, since we said goodbye at your campfire that night."

Noah laughed with delight. "I was the same. It's a little frightening to me." Suddenly she stood away from him and was blushing, looking down. "I hope you don't think I'm too forward!" she said in almost a whisper. "I don't know how to act, Malcham."

He put his hands on her shoulders and pulled her close again, "Don't act, just do what you feel. That's what I'm doing."

He put his arm around her shoulders and they started to walk back toward Asriel and the flock. "We have to talk seriously, Noah. I have come to find out if you will marry me, if I can get your father's consent." He felt her stiffen when he mentioned her father.

"Malcham," she told him sadly, "I believe there is no hope for his ever giving consent."

"Not even if we tell him how much we love each other and I agree to pay him well?" Malcham's heart was sinking. In his talk with his father they had agreed to make a very handsome offer.

"Money and property mean absolutely nothing to him, Malcham; my father is very wealthy. As for love, I think it would delight him to deprive me of love.

"He and my mother loved each other so much that it ended up ruining their lives—and now, ours," she added with a quiver in her voice.

"I have to tell you about my older sister, Mahlah." Noah paused, trying to decide how to tell what had happened and how it had caused her to despair of hope for any of the girls' future.

"You see, Malcham," she began, "I thought my father was refusing matches for me because he was angry at the things I said to him on the day my mother was killed.

"He had gone off to seek an agreement for another wife—knowing that her time of delivery was upon us. I saw my mother get down in the dust at his feet begging him to stay until the baby was born.

"It broke my heart to see her pleading. She knew the baby was a boy. He would not listen. He left us and we fell behind." Noah's voice was trembling as she remembered that awful day.

"We fell behind because the men Father hired ran away as soon as he was gone. Then my mother went into labor. We put her in one of our carts and doubled up again on our duties in moving the animals and household goods.

"Fortunately, the pillar of cloud halted and lowered and we did not become completely separated from the rest. We set up the tent quickly and got help for Mother from our Aunt Hasenuah and some other women.

"My mother had an easy delivery and it was a sweet little boy—hearty and healthy—just as my father had waited for all through the years."

Noah shook her head. "I still find it hard to believe it is true. My mother and the baby were doing so well that I came back to help Asriel and the others with the animals. I was so happy we had a brother! It was going to change all of our lives and we would be a happy family once more. My parents would no longer have to bear the shame of having no male heir. All was going to be well because of this little baby boy.

"But when I went back to check, I found they were both dead and my sisters shocked and grieving. Both my beautiful mother and sweet little Oni had been murdered by the Amalekites."

Malcham was amazed upon hearing the story. He had only known that Zelophehad was a strange and bitter man. He hugged Noah close to his side as they neared Asriel. "I'm so sorry Noah—so sorry! What sad times you have been through. You deserve some happiness and I want to be the one who shares it with you."

Asriel was standing beside his rock waiting for them. He had long since given up on winning Noah. He knew from the very first day of the war games that her heart belonged to this Benjamite. And since Zelophehad refused to let Mahlah marry, it was clear that Noah had no chance to marry anyone.

"Greetings, Malcham!" he said, stepping forward to embrace his Benjamite friend and tutor.

"It is good to see you again," answered, Malcham. He really did like this young cousin of Noah.

"Sit down here in the shadow of my rock," offered Asriel. "Do you want a drink of water? The girls should be here soon with something to eat and we'll share with you."

Asriel had picked up his skin and was offering a drink. Malcham was carrying his own bottle but he accepted Asriel's hospitality. "Thanks," he said, and took a long drink.

The shepherd saw in Noah's face that she would appreciate some time alone with her love. Asriel knew her so well—loved her so well. "You two sit and finish your talk. I'm going out and talk to the sheep," he told them, and picking up his staff, walked away.

Noah looked after him a minute and then went back to what she had intended to tell Malcham about Mahlah. He was waiting quietly for her to begin.

"When Father came back to our camp, he was devastated. He was on his face crying and asking God to forgive him, and I told him it was all his fault. I said something I shouldn't have, but I'm still not sorry, Malcham." There was still defiance in her voice.

"I've known since then that he would find a way to punish me for saying those things. I thought that was the reason he would not consider the offers for me. But I didn't care; I didn't want to marry.

"But then Mahlah found the one she thought God meant for her—or, rather, he found her—and they were so in love! Mahlah has always been the perfectly obedient daughter—always trying her best to please my father.

"He had no reason to refuse Mahlah's Hezron. Hezron is almost as rich as Father and he was willing to give Father any amount he asked. Hezron is a good man with a good family and reputation, and he and Mahlah were so in love. There was absolutely no reason for my father to refuse the match.

"But, Malcham, my father insulted him and threw him out of our tent and warned him not to try to see Mahlah ever again! That was when I knew there could be no hope for me and you."

Malcham was stunned, but he would not give up. "Surely he must have had some reason . . ." he began, hoping to find a difference for Noah and him. But she was absolutely convinced her father would never let her marry.

"No, Malcham," she said with finality in her voice. "He has no reason except he somehow blames us for not being men. That's the cause of all of his troubles and sorrows—he has daughters instead of sons!"

The two young lovers talked on, savoring being together. Time was flying past them. They spoke no more of asking Zelophehad. To Noah, it had been settled when her father had refused Hezron.

They talked about themselves, hurrying to learn all they could about one another before parting again—most likely forever.

Soon Milcah and Tirzah came with the food and Asriel came back to eat with them. The young ones were happy to see the handsome Malcham again. He greeted them heartily and asked them about their songs. He even remembered which one was Milcah and which was Tirzah—they both loved him and thought how fortunate Noah was to have such an admirer and suitor.

Before the girls left, Milcah got up enough courage to ask him to take her greetings to his father and to remind him that he had promised to consider marrying her when she was older.

Malcham, Noah, and Asriel were shocked when they heard this from the usually timid Milcah. Tirzah laughed and nodded her head, confirming it was true.

Then the girls were gone and Asriel removed himself to a distance so the lovers could have the few hours of precious communion left to them before time to take the flock in to water and quarter for the night.

They had talked into the afternoon when they saw Asriel starting to gather the flock. Soon Noah would have to go. "Oh, Malcham, I don't know what I will do without you now." She came into his arms again. "I want you to kiss me so I'll have that to remember as I grow old alone."

She was looking up into his earnest face and closed her eyes, offering her lips for her first kiss. It was so wonderful to Malcham that he almost cried. He kissed her long and tenderly and the thrills went through them both like waves. She just clung to him as he leaned back against her shepherd's rock to steady himself. "How beautiful it is," she cried, "to be loved by the one you love!"

Malcham held her tightly. "Noah, I can't give you up, he said. "No matter what happens, I'm going to ask Zelophehad to let me marry you. I'm going to ask him when he comes to the war games in two months! I just cannot give you up without at least trying to convince him!"

She moved away from him and bowed her head. "I know, I know," she agreed. "But I'm afraid it can't be."

So Malcham walked away once again from his beautiful shepherdess, and she gathered her rod and staff and water bag and hurried after Asriel and the sheep with a heart that was at once rapturously happy and bleakly sorrowful.

Chapter 15

Time drew near for the war games of the tribe of Benjamin. Zelophehad was committed to attend as an observer and adviser representing the tribe of Manesseh, according to the special invitation carried to him last year by the visiting Abdon.

Zelophehad had not attended his own tribe's games, but his family had been well represented by his brothers, Joseph, Machir, and Shemiah, and his nephews, Asriel, Epher, and Shechem.

Zelophehad had consulted with his brothers about making up a party to visit Benjamin for the occasion. All wanted to go, but someone had to stay behind to do the every-day work. It was finally decided, since all the brothers had been involved the year before, that each would send a son.

Machir chose Asriel since he had done so well in the home games the year before. Joseph would send his oldest son, Helek, who had been born about the same time as Zelophehad's Mahlah. Shemiah wanted to send Shechem, who helped with Zelophehad's cattle.

Shemiah chose him because the boy had, as yet, received very little instruction in fighting and needed the experience, but Zelophehad advised he couldn't spare both Asriel and Shechem. Asriel told his father and uncles that he thought it only fair they send Shechem. This cousin was close to Asriel's age but had not yet been allowed to train and participate in these games.

Thus, it was that Zelophehad set off for the Benjamin games with Helek and Shechem. Asriel breathed a sigh of relief at being allowed to remain with his uncle's sheep. He had an idea that something bad might happen at the games and that it would involve Zelophehad.

Zelophehad, himself, seemed more agreeable than he had been since the death of his wife and infant son. He had planned a battle to be played out at the games. He would offer ideas of both an attack and the defense and argue the merits of his plan against the way planners at the games might want to enact it.

Shechem and Helek found him a more agreeable traveling companion than they had anticipated. The three received a warm welcome from the Benjamites.

All the participants in the games were required to sleep out in the open as they would if pursuing a real battle. Zelophehad's plan was well received with lively discussion and then even livelier enactment. It took up most of the day with the two chosen sides giving their recruits special instruction and demonstration in use of various weapons. It was great fun and hard work to the young men and good mental exercise to the fathers and grandfathers.

Abdon was one of the strategists and Malcham was an instructor for the javelin practice. Neither of them had contact with the visiting Manassites.

After the mock battle, the warriors ate and rested. Then the races and contests were held. After night fell, a celebration and honors program began that lasted into the night.

Malcham had waited patiently, trying to find a convenient time to approach Zelophehad, who was sitting with a group of Benjamite leaders. When no opportunity to speak privately to him presented itself, he approached the group and asked if the could ask the visiting adviser a question. He was being very polite and respectful.

"Sirs, it is of a rather personal nature, but I have no other way to ask than here and now."

The Benjamite leaders asked Zelophehad if he would like to step aside and talk to the young warrior alone. Zelophehad felt he had seen this young man before, and was suspicious, but also curious.

"No," he said, "let him ask."

Malcham stepped closer and spoke in a low tone that only those closest could hear. "Sir, I wish to ask for your daughter, Noah in marriage. I am offering . . ." Zelophehad leapt to his feet and shouted, "No! She cannot marry! The answer is no to you and no to anyone else." His eyes were blazing.

All the onlookers were astonished at this outburst.

Malcham did not step back, but asked in the same quiet voice, "Sir, may I ask what reason . . .?"

"No!" The enraged man shouted again. "I don't have to give a reason. She is my daughter." He started menacingly toward the stricken young Benjamite.

Abdon and several others quickly stepped up and led Malcham away.

Then Zelophehad addressed all those present, "I repeat, I will not allow my daughters to marry," he said in a loud, deliberate voice. "Now, we must leave. Thank you for your hospitality and goodnight." He motioned his two nephews to follow and walked away from the Benjamite camp.

Part II

Chapter 1

The wanderings of Israel in the wilderness continued. Year after year Moses obeyed God's command and led Israel to follow their guiding pillar. The old, disobedient generation, which had refused to enter into The Land, was dying off. New sons and daughters of Abraham were being born to replace them.

Four daughters of Zelophehad continued to serve their father as hired servants might. Mahlah, Noah, Milcah, and Tirzah received no wages and no evident gratitude from him.

Hoglah lived on happily in her adopted family of Reubenites. She had matured gracefully and was a great help and source of delight to her new parents. Her "brothers" were also maturing. Hanock and Pallu, the two older, had been betrothed and were preparing homes to receive their brides and leave their parental nest.

Hoglah had received attention and inquiries for marriage from several families in the passing years. But when Reuben and Anthah brought the offers to her, she told them she had no desire to marry and leave them. The parents and younger brothers were happy to keep her in their loving presence.

One day, led by the pillar, Israel came up to the border of the land of Edom—the country God had given to the descendants of Esau, Israel's brother. Moses sent in messengers asking Edom to allow them to pass through their land. He promised that his people would not enter the fields or vineyards, would not drink the water of the wells, but would only go through by the king's highway without turning to the right or to the left until they had all passed the borders.

Edom sent an answer threatening to come out to fight against them if they tried to enter. Israel asked again, promising to pay for water they or their cattle might drink. Again, the answer was, "Thou shalt not go through." Then they came out armed to prevent Israel's passage—so Israel had to turn away.

God had warned Moses about Esau's land. He said Israel was not to meddle with Edom. He said He would not give Israel their land—not so much as a foot breadth—because He had given mount Seir to Esau for a possession.

Also, God admonished Moses not to distress or contend with the Moabites in battle. Israel was not to have their land because God had given it to the children of Lot.

One day men from the tribe of Levi spread out walking through the whole camp of the Israelites announcing to one and all that Aaron, their high priest, had died and Eleazar, his oldest remaining son, had been anointed by Moses, at the instruction of God, to be the new high priest. There was to be a period of mourning for Aaron lasting thirty days.

The day the Levites came through his part of the camp with the news about Aaron, Zelophehad invited them into his tent for food and drink and they gladly accepted his hospitality.

Mahlah, Milcah and Tirzah performed the welcome and set extra places at the noon meal.

The whole of Israel was experiencing strange stirrings and excitement still from the encounter and turning away of Israel by Edom. There was anticipation in the air, a sense that something important was about to take place. The routine in which they had lived so long had been slightly disrupted and they had been left with a feeling of more to come.

These Levites could not stay long, but were grateful for the shade of their host's tent and the attendance of his gracious daughters. The conversation as they dined was about how God had instructed Moses to take Aaron and Eleazar up to mount Hor in the sight of all the congregation. God had told Moses that Aaron was to die there and not be allowed to enter into the land He had promised to Irsael because of Aaron's rebellion against God at Meribah.

Moses was to strip him of his holy garments there on the mount and put them on Eleazar. Then Aaron died there and Moses and Eleazar returned to the camp to tell the people Israel was to mourn for Aaron thirty days.

This was, indeed, another big change for Israel. The man Aaron had been their high priest for as long as the priesthood had existed. Drastic change!

Zelophehad and the daughters were still digesting this news when the Levites thanked them and left them and hurried on their way through the camps of the tribes with their news and the order of the thirty days of mourning.

Milcah and Tirzah, who were now grown young ladies, could hardly wait to take the news out to the shepherds. When they told Asriel and Noah, their cousin seemed to make more of it than they or their father had thought. "You know," Asriel told them, "this is important. Things are beginning to happen that might lead us right into our new land. I believe those of us who will be army should keep ourselves ready to fight at an instant's notice."

Noah and her sisters took what Asriel said seriously. He was a mature man now and skilled in the arts of fighting. His family had tried several times to persuade him to take a wife, but he couldn't give up being with Noah—even if it was just working together.

He told the girls, "I believe that soon we will receive word that Moses needs so many men to go out and fight for all of us."

Noah agreed. "Who do you think we'll be fighting?" she asked Asriel, knowing that he had more contact with people who talked about what was going on. The young shepherd looked at his cousins who depended mostly upon him for their outside information. "There's really no way to guess which nation will resist us or when they might do it," he told them.

"We are surrounded by all these different nations and they all would like to see us beaten and driven out. You can be sure it won't be Edom because they know God doesn't want us to bother them. The same applies to Moab and Ammon who are related to us. But, we are close to the southern Canaanites and also to Midian. It might be any one from the land around us. But we're surely going to fight."

"Will you go?" Tirzah asked him. The younger girls loved Asriel. He was kind and agreeable to them—more like a father than the morose, unhappy Zelophehad.

"I want to go," he said. "If I am chosen I will go."

Noah's thoughts were about another young warrior so dear in her memory. She had not seen Malcham since his visit before the games in Benjamin five years ago. But he had sent word to her by travelers and hunters now and then.

It was a very unsatisfactory way to communicate your love, but it was the only thing available. He dared not try to see her because of the extreme reaction he saw in her father to his asking for her hand in marriage. He was sure Zelophehad was capable of violence if provoked. But he had not given up on the hope that he would some day marry Noah.

Not long after the thirty days of mourning for Aaron the high priest had been completed and Israel was on the march again, Noah's question to Asriel about which people they would be fighting was answered. The Levites passed through the hosts once again. This time they came to alert the fighting men. Each of the tribes was to send men to battle the Canaanites.

Their king, Arad, had heard of Israel's approach and he sent his army to attack and took some prisoners. Moses and the leaders had vowed unto the LORD that if He would deliver these Canaanites into Israel's hands they would destroy all their cities.

Excitement mounted throughout the camps as the leaders of each tribe decided who was to go to battle and sent them off to Moses to quickly form an army.

Asriel was chosen to go. Milcah and Tirzah were sent out to replace him as shepherds.

Mahlah, Noah, and the younger girls were very fond of Asriel and dreaded to see him go, but they were also very proud of him as he marched off with the others of the tribe of Manasseh to perform the vow Israel had made to utterly destroy the cities of the Canaanites as the LORD delivered them into their hands.

They won battle after battle and destroyed Arad and his people and their cities.

When Asriel returned, he was expected to tell about the heroic feats he and his comrades had accomplished—as he had once told about the war games. But Asriel was not the same. He wouldn't talk about the battles. And, when pressed, he would only say that the LORD had been with him and the other warriors of Israel and that all credit and praise should be given to Him.

After these battles and the destruction of the Canaanites, people again began their complaining against Moses. Now Israel journeyed from mount Hor by way of the Red Sea to go around the land that belonged to Edom. Israel was very discouraged because of the long "detour."

The complaining started with the mixed multitude—people who were Egyptians intermarried with Israelites—and spread throughout the camps. People were complaining and speaking against Moses—and even against God.

They complained about everything—especially about the lack of water, and one even dared to say his soul loathed the manna. It wasn't long before it seemed almost everyone was complaining about the manna.

Zelophehad's daughters did not complain. They loved manna and knew many different ways to prepare it. They liked it best just the way God sent it to them and they realized complaining about it was complaining against God.

Then serpents began to appear in the camps and people were bitten. Victims of the "fiery serpents" were the ones who had been complaining. They did not die immediately, but suffered for days before finally succumbing to the intense, fiery pain that seemed to spread through their whole body.

Their loved ones had no idea how to treat them—no idea of what, if anything, might relieve such agony that slowly sapped the strength. The fiery pain would come over the sufferer in waves and cause muscle spasms that lasted several minutes, then left him weak and gasping for breath and praying to die before being seized by the next wave.

Milcah, Tirzah, and Mahlah, like the others in the camps, encountered these serpents everywhere. The creatures would suddenly appear from under tent furnishings, or in the sand in the spaces between the tents, or in the paths leading to the outskirts of the camps—anywhere and everywhere.

They seemed to choose their prey—some people were bitten—some seemed to escape their attack over and over. The girls spent a lot of time killing the serpents that invaded their tent and the environs. They were easily killed with a rock or a heavy stick. What made them so frightening was the way they appeared suddenly—seemingly out of thin air.

Asriel and Noah and other shepherds reported rarely seeing a serpent while they tended the flock. The fiery serpents seemed to prefer the areas in and around the tents.

Death toll from their bites began to mount. People stopped complaining and some began to pray.

One morning Mahlah woke and began her routine of waking Milcah and Tirzah and preparing to go out to gather the day's manna. Usually, Zelophehad was awake before his daughters and had been outside the tent before any of them came out—always coming back to call them all to help him gather. This morning Mahlah waited several minutes, hesitating to go out to look for him, so as not to break their routine or appear to be taking charge. Finally, she told her waiting sisters, "Something is wrong. I believe we should go to look for Father." And they all had an idea of what was delaying him.

They stood waiting, fearing to go outside. Finally, Tirzah stepped to the door of the tent and the others followed. They took separate ways and each had taken only a few steps when Milcah came upon Zelophehad lying in the space between their own tent and their next door neighbors. He was writhing in silent agony, muscles convulsing with the waves of indescribable pain. Coiled next to him was a fiery serpent, the creature that had inflicted this awful suffering. It seemed to be watching him. Milcah picked up a rock and smashed its head.

She called to the others, "Here he is! I have found Father!"

The two came running. As they reached Milcah, Zelophehad's spasm relaxed and he said weakly, "Carry me into the tent and then go gather the manna for today."

They obeyed as always. Everyone in the camp knew by now, there was nothing they could do for the people who had been bitten. It was just a matter of waiting on death.

They carried Zelophehad—Mahlah and Tirzah at his head and under his arms and Milcah at his feet—into the tent and laid him upon his sleeping mat.

Another serpent came slithering as they were putting him down. It did not attack; it seemed to want to just look at Zelophehad. Milcah dropped her father's feet and snatched up a wooden paddle to strike it a killing blow.

Mahlah propped her father's head and shoulders with the decorated pillows and Milcah spread his sleeping cover over him.

"Go gather the day's food," he ordered again. So they left him and took their pots and went out into the bright morning knowing this was the beginning of death for their father.

Zelophehad's daughters tended him day and night. They set up a schedule of when each would sit by his bed and when each would sleep and when each would be doing her household chores.

The daughter in attendance would feed him by hand, having propped him in a sitting position against the many pillows used for sitting while entertaining. After the first five days, he started to refuse food. His digestive tract was on fire and he only wanted to die and have done with it.

For the first two nights he had regained enough strength to hobble outside to relieve himself, supported on either side by a strong young daughter, one of whom carried the paddle to dig the hole and then cover it when he had finished. But by the third night he was too weak to travel even that short distance.

Milcah then took one of their clay pots and set it upon one of the sturdier reed boxes and he used that instead. This then had to be carried out and emptied and washed or thrown into a hole and covered. These pots were disposable, if need be.

But when the convulsive spasms seized him, he would also lose bowel and bladder control. Then the daughter on duty would wash him and change the soiled bedclothes, throwing the dirty linen into a water pot outside the front door of the tent.

Zelophehad said nothing, but all this was deeply humiliating to a strong man in his prime, who only a few days before had been in control of his whole world.

A fire was kept under the dirty linen pot in the daytime. Another pot for rinsing sat nearby. This meant carrying water. The soiled linen was washed daily and hung over a line stretched between two poles. This sight was to be found duplicated over and over throughout the tribal camps.

This work, for the most part was performed by servants, but Mahlah, Milcah, and Hoglah had no servants and were accustomed to lowly tasks. They labored faithfully without complaining. The one who sat with Zelophehad stayed awake and alert throughout her eight hours and gave him water when he wanted—offering it often.

She did not try to converse with him, but after one of the frequent paroxysms and the washing and linen changes, would gently bathe his face with a clean, cool damp cloth. No one could have been cared for with more tenderness.

He grew weaker by the day and seemed to wither away before their eyes. Tirzah, Milcah, and Mahlah had very little occasion to speak with each other, but when they did speak, they did not discuss their father.

The whole of Israel was in crisis brought on by their continual complaining. God had finally decided it was enough and had sent judgment in the form of the serpents. Almost every activity had come to a halt as families ministered to the stricken and then began to bury the dead.

They were vulnerable on all sides, but their enemies were not aware of the situation.

The leaders of the tribes hurried to Moses with pleas from their constituents. The message was repeated over and over.

" . . . We have sinned for, we have spoken against the LORD, and against thee; pray unto the LORD, that he take away the serpents from us . . ." (Numbers 21:7 KJV)

And Moses prayed once again for the people. This time the LORD gave him surprising orders:

". . . Make thee a fiery serpent, and set it upon a pole: and it shall come to pass, that everyone that is bitten, when he looketh upon it, shall live." (Numbers 21:8 KJV) Moses hurried to carry out God's order. He cast a serpent of molten brass. (Made from the same stash of material as the brazen altar and the brazen laver that stood in the outer court of the tabernacle.) He fashioned it with a graving tool until it was an exact replica of the serpents wreaking havoc among his people and he set it up on a pole outside the front gate of the tabernacle for all to see.

He then dispatched messengers to go through the camps with the message, "Come, look, and live!"

God kept his word. If a victim would only look to the serpent of brass—no matter how close to death he was—instantly healed.

Chapter 2

On the ninth day since being bitten, Zelophehad was near death. The men Moses had sent out with the good news of the brass serpent had not yet reached his part of the camp. The girls were continuing their faithful care and duties. Early in the afternoon, Mahlah was busy at the front of their tent, punching down and stirring the boiling pot of linens from the bed. She then notified Tirzah it was time to help her wring them and transfer them to the rinse, then wring them again and hang them on the line.

Mahlah was wet with perspiration from the heat of the fire. She paused to wipe her brow before summoning Tirzah. At that moment she saw her Uncle Joseph approaching. He was followed by two menservants carrying a litter upon which lay the wasted remains of what had once been his robust wife and her aunt, Hasenuah. Mahlah did not recognize her at once, but knew that the person there was a serpent victim.

Joseph embraced Mahlah and asked, "Who has been bitten, Mahlah?"

"It is Father," she said. "He has been suffering nine days, now. Who is that on the litter? Where are you going?"

Her uncle's expression was very serious. "It is your Aunt Hasenuah. She was also bitten nine days ago. I think she is near death. Is Zelophehad conscious? Is he rational? We need to talk to him—and to you girls. It is very important and I don't know how much time we have."

Mahlah was alarmed. "What is it, Uncle Joseph? I think Father is awake. He never talks with us, so it is hard to know when he is awake."

Joseph spoke again with urgency. "Get your sisters together as quickly as possible. Is Noah still with the sheep? Send for her. Finish what you are doing as quickly as you can and come in to us and Zelophehad."

He motioned for the men to carry Hasenuah into the tent and followed the litter inside.

Mahlah called through the doorway to Tirzah, "Come quickly, and tell Milcah to come help me finish here!"

A startled Tirzah came out of the tent, looking back at the ones who had just entered, and almost bumped into the two men who had just walked into their tent space.

"Is this the tent of Zelophehad?" one of them asked.

"It is," said Tirzah politely, "can I help you?"

"We were summoned by Joseph to meet him here. I am your judge and this man is one of your tribal elders. Joseph said it is important."

Mahlah came to the men. "My father, Zelophehad, was bitten by one of the fiery serpents. He is near death."

"Joseph has asked us to meet with them," the man said.

Mahlah moved out of the way. "Go on in," she said. She turned to Tirzah. "Go in and send Milcah out to help me. Then run quickly and bring Noah back with you." Tirzah followed the men into the tent in time to hear Joseph say to Zelophehad, "I am sorry you are ill, brother. When your girls all get here you must wake enough to hear what we have to tell you. But rest until then." He spoke softly, patting Zelophehad's claw-like hand.

Zelophehad stared at the intruders but said nothing.

Tirzah delivered Mahlah's message to Milcah and asked, "Who is that on the litter?" Milcah stood and walked to the door with her. "It is our Aunt Hasenuah; she has also been bitten by the serpent."

"I guessed that, but didn't know who it was," Tirzah called back as she started off for the shepherds at a run. Mahlah and Milcah turned the boiling wash pot over with their heavy sticks causing the water to extinguish the fire. They were experts at directing the water onto the fire while avoiding the splash. Then they picked the wet linens from the pot with the sticks, waving them in the air to cool them and throwing them back to pick up the next and the next and repeat until all the pieces were cool enough to handle.

They took the pieces one by one by the ends and twisted in opposite directions to wring them and throw them into the rinse water. They stirred and punched them in the large rinse water pot until they were satisfied they'd rinsed out all of the wash water they possibly could. Then, taking them out one at a time, they repeated the wringing process and hung them on the line to dry.

They were finishing when Noah and Tirzah came running up to them. Tirzah bent over from the waist, trying to get her breath back. "What is happening?" Noah asked. "Tirzah wouldn't tell me anything except I've been ordered to appear before Uncle Joseph and an elder and a judge." Her eyes were wide with excitement. "What has father blamed me for now?"

Mahlah and Milcah looked at each other and couldn't help but giggle. "Oh Noah, it's not you—don't worry. We don't know what it is about, but we'll soon find out. Let's all go in now," said the oldest, smoothing her hair and starting for the door.

The daughters of Zelophehad filed into the tent in order of age. They stood beside their father's bed and waited.

There was a heavy silence in the tent. Everyone was looking to Joseph except Noah who was staring down into the gaunt face of Zelophehad. The men who had carried Hasenuah's litter had set it down parallel to where Zelophehad lay.

Noah looked from one serpent bite victim to the other. She had not seen before what the bites could do and she was horrified at the change in her father and aunt.

Joseph was hesitating, dreading to begin the terrible thing he had to do. He looked at his older brother who had once been so virile and handsome; Zelophehad was now just a shell. Joseph prayed there was still enough life left in that shell to comprehend what he was to hear this day.

Joseph looked at his nieces—how dear they were to him—and how good they had been to this father who treated them so badly He knew very little of the details, but he knew they had cruelly suffered in their short lives.

The judge and the elder were looking expectantly to him; he knew he had to get on with his business. He drew a deep breath and said to his menservants, "Please wait for me outside the tent."

The two men left. They had no idea why their master had uprooted his fatally ill wife and brought her here to his brother's home. They were curious and would have loved to stay and listen. Maybe they would be able to hear from outside. They would certainly try.

Joseph began, "Brother, can you hear me?" he asked Zelophehad, bending over the bed. Zelophehad's eyes opened and looked up into all the surrounding faces. His gaze stopped and stayed on Noah's face and his expression turned to a scowl.

"Do you hear me?" Joseph repeated.

The sunken black eyes moved to Joseph. "Yes, I hear you, Joseph. What do you want?" His voice was strong. Everyone in the tent was surprised.

Joseph said, "Brother, my wife has been bitten by one of the fiery serpents. She knows she is dying and there is something she has to tell you." Zelophehad's eyes opened wider and he searched the faces above him. He did not see Hasenuah's face among them.

Joseph realized that his brother did not see the litter beside him. "She is here, beside you, Zelophehad." He turned to Mahlah. "Can you raise him to a sitting position?"

Mahlah and Milcah lifted their father and leaned him forward from the waist. Tirzah deftly arranged several of the beautiful big pillows behind him to support his back. He grimaced, but did not make a sound.

Noah still stared. *Oh, how he has changed!*

Joseph knelt beside Hasenuah and raised her to almost a sitting position. He supported her back against him so that she and Zelophehad were positioned face to face. He looked up and told the judge and the elder and his nieces, "Please listen closely. My wife knows she is dying and that she has done a great wrong against God and against this family. This is her confession. Her voice is weak—so listen!"

Hasenuah had not opened her eyes until this moment. When she did, they could see there was still a lot more life in her than they had guessed. Still she did not speak.

Joseph waited again, and in an effort to help her to start, he declared, "Since Zelophehad's refusal to marry Hasenuah when his parents made arrangements for them long ago, she has harbored a resentment which has festered and caused this unspeakable thing to come about. "Tell them, Hasenuah." He gave his wife a gentle shake.

This introduction fed the interest of the listeners; they all leaned closer.

Hasenuah's eyes burned brightly as she looked into the eyes of Zelophehad, which were riveted upon her face. "You greatly humiliated me," she told him. "No one knows how shamed I was at your refusal to honor what your parents and mine wanted." She paused and swallowed twice and tears began to form in her sunken eyes and run down her prominent, bony cheeks.

"I felt as if you had wiped your feet on me. When our parents then decided on matching me with Joseph, I agreed and tried to be a good wife, but always I have felt that the inherited firstborn rights and privileges belong to my son, Helek, because if you had married me as agreed, he would have—should have been your son!"

Hasenuah fell back against Joseph's sturdy chest and closed her eyes again. This was taking all the strength she could muster.

Zelophehad seemed to garner strength from somewhere and leaned forward to make sure he was hearing every word. "What are you saying, Hasenuah? Tell us what you have done," he cried. He was remembering all the different little subtle ways this sister-in-law had lauded her superiority to Naronah in the matter of producing sons. At those times he had been so grief stricken over his little premature and stillborn sons, he had paid no attention to her or anyone else, but now he remembered clearly the actions of a woman scorned.

She opened her eyes and began to speak again. Joseph was weeping softly as he supported the ruined body of the woman he had loved since their marriage. He had always known of her jealousy and resentment of Zelophehad's Naronah. She had succeeded in covering it to a certain extent to others, but he had known all along. He was completely crushed when she finally told him what this envy and malice had led her to do.

"These feelings have dominated my life," she said. "I actually rejoiced when your babies died. I felt it vindicated me!"

Zelophehad's eyes widened in horror. An idea of where this was leading was forming in the back of his consciousness. "What have you done, Hasenuah?" he demanded.

She began to sob and forced herself to get the whole thing out. "When you left Naronah that day to go to seek a new wife, the men you hired left her and ran away. She and the girls managed to stay fairly close to their place in the march. But then she went into labor and they had to stop and rearrange things and get her into a cart.

"By the time the cloud pillar stopped and lowered, they were far behind—almost on the outer edge of the march. They hurried and succeeded in setting up the tent. Naronah was well into labor.

"Mahlah sent Hoglah to bring me and the other women to help deliver the baby. The girls had to help tend the cattle and sheep and other livestock and do all the work the men who ran away had been hired to do.

"Naronah had no difficulty in the birth and a little baby boy came forth—perfect and healthy. We left them alone for a short time while we went to check on our family duties." Hasenuah was panting for breath, gathering more strength to get through what she had to tell. Her eyes moved up to her nieces who had always respected her. They were all crying, remembering the day she was telling about.

"Oh God, forgive me! I went back earlier than the others. Naronah was dead—run through with the spear of an Amalekite. But that sweet baby boy was alive—unharmed.

"Something had frightened the killers away and they had dropped one of their arrows. I looked at the baby and somehow I saw in him all my humiliation and imagined loss. I thought if he were dead like his brothers, the inheritance would rightly go to my sons. I picked up the arrow and stabbed him through his little heart!"

Hasenuah fell back against the weeping Joseph and he lowered her to the litter and remained there on his knees, head bowed.

Everyone who had heard this ghastly account was horrified. The girls turned to each other, weeping. Mahlah almost collapsed and Noah held her in a strong embrace. Milcah and Tirzah clung to each other as always, and sobbed.

Zelophehad stared at Joseph and his wife for another moment and then fell back against his pillows.

The man who had identified himself as a judge waited a few minutes and when no one spoke, he said to Joseph, "Why did you ask us to come?"

Joseph got to his feet. "I just wanted official witness to my wife's confession to the murder of Zelophehad's son and these girls' brother. I don't know how it would apply, but I wanted the truth to be noted and used in whatever might come up in future dealings with my brother's inheritance."

The elder said, "It is duly noted and we will attest to it in writing for any future reference." He looked at the shrunken figures on the litter and the bed and then at the sorrowing girls. He could think of nothing he or the judge could do to help. "We will go now," he told Joseph and they quietly left the tent.

Joseph stood with shoulders slumped and said to Zelophehad and his daughters, "I am so sorry."

Zelophehad opened his eyes once more and said, "You go now!"

Joseph went to the door and summoned the men to carry the litter. As they carried Hasenuah out the door, men were running through the camp shouting, "If you have been bitten by the serpents go quickly to the tabernacle and look upon the brass serpent raised up there. You will be healed! Look to the brass serpent and be healed!"

Chapter 3

A great stir in the camp followed the men who brought the good news about the brazen serpent. It was hope! There had been no hope before. It sounded too good to be true, but the men who had brought the promise had also brought eye witness accounts of dying people simply believing and acting on God's instructions and being instantly healed.

After Joseph and the men carrying Hasenuah left the tent, the daughters of Zelophehad could hear the sounds of growing excitement and activity. Their father lay on his pillows, eyes closed, and face expressionless.

They tried to collect themselves—each wondering what effect this confession would have on their lives. It had reopened the old wounds of the loss of their mother and inflicted a new wound of betrayal by the aunt they had trusted all these years without their mother.

But they had learned during the long six years to be strong—and that they could depend on each other—and that, certainly, was reassuring as they grew more aware of the bustle outside.

They dried their tears and looked at each other with the question, *what should we do now?* in their eyes. Noah spoke, "First thing we should do is find out what is happening out there." She led the way to the door.

People all around them were already making litters to carry the serpent victims to the tabernacle. Time was of the essence and they figured carrying them this way would be faster than an ox cart. Few of the victims would be strong enough to ride the distance on a donkey. It was a puzzling sight to the girls who had heard the noise, but not the message that the men had brought from God.

They stood outside watching people working and running about. Finally, Noah stopped a woman who was passing the tent and asked, "What is happening?" "Didn't you hear the good news the men brought from Moses?" the woman asked.

"No, we were in the tent and missed them. What is the good news?"

The woman repeated God's promise of life if the dying would obey His instruction and look to the brazen serpent. Noah and her sisters thought there must be more to it than that.

Mahlah said, "Surely that's not all one would have to do."

The woman answered her, "That's what I thought, too. But they swore they saw people instantly made well when they did as God directed Moses." With that, the woman hurried on her way.

Milcah said quietly, "We must get Father to the brazen serpent."

"Oh, that's right!" Mahlah agreed. "And we must hurry. I don't think he has much longer." She started back to the tent and Milcah and Tirzah were close behind, when Noah, standing still in her place called after them, "Don't you think we had better get some help from Asriel and Ishi—and the brothers? The tabernacle is a long way from here."

They all stopped again. "Father's lost a lot of his weight," Mahlah told her.

"That's still a long way to carry any weight and we'll need to go as fast as possible," added Milcah.

"I think we are going to need some help from the men this time, Mahlah," Tirzah said.

"I suppose you are right. But, let us go and tell Father the good news first. He may have his own ideas about how best to get there."

Noah shrugged and followed them into the tent.

To their utter amazement, Zelophehad was sitting up looking toward the tent door waiting their return. He reached out to Mahlah as she neared the bed. "Daughter, do we have some manna left from this morning's gathering?" he asked. His voice was weak.

The girls exchanged glances dreading what might be coming next. "Yes, Father, we always gather enough for three meals." She looked to her sisters again.

Zelophehad smiled! "I believe I should eat a bowl of manna with some milk."

Mahlah and the two youngest sisters all smiled back at their patient who had not eaten in days. Noah just stared.

"Do you really mean it, Father?" asked Tirzah. Zelophehad smiled at her, too. "Yes, I really mean it, little one."

Tirzah was filled with delight. This was the first time she had ever heard him use an endearing term addressing her. She knelt down and took his hand and looked into his eyes. The large dark eyes were smiling at her, too—and he didn't remove his big hand from her small one. "Tirzah, how pretty you have grown," he exclaimed. "All of you are beautiful and good," he said looking up to the startled faces of the other three. I wonder what Hoglah looks like now, I always thought she looked more like your mother than any of you."

They drew in their breath in unbelieving surprise. Mahlah turned away with tears in her eyes. "I'll get the manna for you," she told him, and hurried to the other side of the tent where the food was stored. Her eyes were clouding up with tears again. *Could it be that God has given us back our father?* she thought.

Tirzah was chattering away to Zelophehad, telling him about the men sent from Moses and God and the good news.

 Zelophehad received the bowl from Mahlah's hand and asked, "Is that all they said to do?" Like everyone else, he found it hard to believe.

Noah spoke to him for the first time, "They said only look and live! They also said they had witnessed dying people made well instantly by obeying God's instructions." She waited for the expected scowl to appear on her father's face, but when he looked at her, he smiled. He was eating the manna as if he would never quit eating.

Tirzah said, "Father, we are going to take you to the brazen serpent. We are going to use a litter because it will be the fastest way to go. We decided that we will have to ask the men to carry you so you will get there as soon as possible. One of us will go along, but let the men carry you. The others can relieve the men on their jobs while you are gone."

Mahlah interrupted, "This is just what we thought, Father. We came to ask you how you would have us get you there."

Zelophehad finished the bowl of manna. It had not yet started to burn his stomach. "Please give me a drink of water,' he asked Milcah, who poured from the pot, they kept by his bed, into his cup and handed it to him. *Oh father,* she thought, *why did you wait until you are dying?*

He drank the whole cup and said, "Thank you all for caring for me so lovingly! I couldn't ask for better daughters!" He knew another paroxysm was long overdue. He lay back against the pillows to rest and ready himself for the terrible pain and burning fire.

He closed his eyes again.

"Father," Mahlah said gently. "We need to hurry to get you to the brass serpent. You are very near death and I don't know how much time we have."

 He opened his eyes again. "Do you think our plan is the right one?" asked Milcah. "Shall I run to ask Asriel, Ishi, Jahdiel and Eliel to come? We can be making the litter from tent poles and bed covers."

Zelophehad began to convulse. His back bowed, his head was drawn back, and his arms and legs drew up and shook violently. All they could do was wait until this storm passed. Noah had not witnessed this before and she gave a little cry and turned away nauseated.

Finally, the shaking ceased and the neck, back, arms, and legs relaxed. Noah watched as her sisters worked together to remove the urine soaked clothes from their humbled father. The bowels had not moved this time since they were empty from days without food.

Milcah and Mahlah turned his emaciated body and washed him and slipped clean linens under as they pulled out the soiled ones. Tirzah bathed his face with a damp cloth.

Finally they turned him back and covered him with another cloth. Tears were coming out of the corners of his eyes. "How could you?" they heard him whisper, and all leaned toward him. "How could you still treat me so tenderly after what I've done to you?"

"You are our father!" Milcah answered for all of them.

"I am so sorry, my girls. God forgive me, I am so sorry! Now I don't have time to make it up to you!" His voice grew a little stronger.

Tirzah knelt beside him and put her arm across his chest and around his neck and leaned her head next to his. "I love you, Father," she told him. "I always have and I always will."

Noah spoke again with urgency. "We need to get you to brass serpent, Father. Shall I run to get the men?"

"I don't think we have time to make it," Zelophehad said weakly, stroking Tirzah's shining hair. "I want to spend what time I have left with you. I am ready to go on and be with you dear mother and little Oni. I only wish Hoglah was here! Poor little girl. She was so frightened." The tears were starting again. "I know now that she must have seen what happened and had no one in which to confide, someone who would protect her. How could I have failed all of you so miserably?

"I want you to know you have never once failed me. I am so proud to be your father!"

They all protested. "At least let us try to get you there, Father," Mahlah begged. "Then we would have the rest of your life for catching up on what we've missed."

"I am just too tired, Mahlah. I ate that manna to try to gain enough strength to last long enough to tell you all these things and to let you know I do love you!"

"Please, Father, please," Noah asked, "let us take you to be healed." Noah surprised herself. She realized how much she still loved her father and wanted to be close to him again as she had once been. "We have so many things to straighten out."

Zelophehad closed his eyes again. "No, Noah," he said with finality. "I need these last hours to talk about business with you. I am so weary now, girls, I want to sleep. Let me sleep again and you rest. We'll talk more when I wake."

They did as he asked. All of them sat by the bed and as he woke again they talked about everything he thought they needed to know to carry on when he was gone. He told them where his gold and silver and precious jewels were kept. He told them to go to Joseph for the division of the livestock. "He is a good man; he will deal honestly and truthfully with you!"

He would drift gently off to sleep again and they still sat by. Mahlah prepared their evening meal and they ate sitting next to his bed.

Zelophehad had more convulsions and went back to sleep after each of them. When he roused again they talked about what the girls wanted to tell him. They each accepted his decision to die peacefully at home and they told him they forgave him. They were so happy to see him at peace. All of them were happier than they had been in many years.

Milcah and Tirzah experienced ever so briefly the joy of having a loving and approving father. They were so full of joy they were glowing.

He told Mahlah and Noah that he more than approved their marriage toHezron and Malcham. "They are brave young men who loved you enough and didn't hesitate to face me and ask for you! Contact them and marry and know that I bless the union."

He woke once more long after dark had settled over the camp. It was unusually quiet since so many had left to take serpent victims to the brazen serpent. Noah had lit one small oil lamp and the girls dozed now and then, awaiting the next awakening of their father. They looked at each other and smiled now and then. Peace permeated the large tent of Zelophehad.

When he woke the final time, he spoke to Tirzah, "Will you and Milcah do one last thing for me?" His voice was stronger again and peace shone from his eyes.

"We will do any thing we can, Father," Tirzah answered eagerly. "What do you want?" Milcah moved closer. They were so pleased he wanted something they could give. He looked at these two who were so close to each other and had so much love to give—and he was full of regret for having rejected them all these years. He was surprised that he actually knew a lot more about them than he thought.

He smiled again. "Will you sing for me?"

They looked at each other in absolute delight. "Oh yes, we would love to—what would you like us to sing?"

"I once heard you singing a song about an eagle," Zelophehad told them. "I loved both the melody and the words. You made it all, didn't you, Milcah.

I think it is wonderful—another thing for me to be proud about. Can you sing it for me now?"

"Oh yes, Father, thank you!" Milcah said.

Tirzah began, "Oh strong and mighty eagle" and Milcah joined on the third note. They sang their very best for him and as they finished, "If I could fly—if I could fly," Zelophehad went to sleep for the last time.

Chapter 4

Mahlah, Noah, Milcah, and Tirzah slowly adjusted their lives to being without Zelophehad. Their communion with him the last hours of his life had healed their hearts of much of the hurt endured during the years when he desperately yearned for a son. They found their riches hidden away among his personal things exactly as he had told them. And they consulted with their grieving and contrite uncle, Joseph, about their livestock. He was more than accommodating in helping them to find exactly which and how many animals belonged to them. He felt responsible and went out of his way to try to restore some of the happiness they had lost with the death of their little baby brother, Oni.

Joseph was a sensitive man and had not been blind to the unfairness to which these girls had been subjected for years. In the case of the two younger, it had been all they had ever known.

He talked with the four about what was theirs. He took them and showed them the cattle, goats, and donkeys that Epher, Shechem, Ishi, and the brothers, Eliel and Jahiel tended for them. He had his sons meet with the girls and made sure each knew what belonged to them.

They were familiar with the tending of the sheep so needed no instruction on that account.

It surprised him somewhat when he learned that Mahlah and Milcah were the ones who were interested and able and eager to learn the management side of Zelophehad's wealth. He devoted time to showing and telling them what they needed to know and to do as the occasion arose.

Another great source of help was their cousin, Asriel. He still faithfully cared for their sheep. Noah continued her shepherding and Milcah now spent full time at that chore since there was much less to do at the tent—Mahlah and Tirzah needed no help.

Asriel would not leave the beloved sisters. He knew he should have been married long ago and begun a family of his own. But his heart still belonged to Noah and he was too honest to pretend to love someone else.

With the death of Zelophehad, he had experienced a small flicker of hope once again. They had not heard from Malcham for some time. *Could it be that he had given in to pressure to produce the next generation and married someone else?* Asriel rejected the idea. Malcham was as true as he, himself; Asriel knew he would be waiting for Noah.

Noah had told him, as he was dying, Zelophehad had given his blessing to both Mahlah's marriage to Hezron and her marriage to Malcham. Asriel had no idea why, but he became convinced that he should be the one to take this news to Malcham.

As their lives settled into a routine once again his conscience was reminding him daily that he should go and tell.

Joseph knew that Asriel was as devoted to his nieces as anyone they would ever be likely to find. He also observed Asriel had matured into a capable and reliable man. He spoke to Mahlah and Tirzah about making Asriel the overseer of all their possessions (taking Zelophehad's place in that capacity) and hiring someone else to tend the sheep.

The girls agreed this was a good idea and consulted with Milcah and Noah who also agreed someone was needed, and could think of no one who could better fill that position.

Israel had not moved since the death of their father, but once the pillar lifted, a person who was familiar with all aspects of what the girls owned would be needed to supervise the preparation and then the moving along with the rest of Israel.

One morning, soon after Joseph brought up the subject, Mahlah and Tirzah were with Noah and Milcah when they arrived to relieve Asriel attending the flock. Asriel saw them coming and was ready to greet them with a smile of genuine pleasure. He enjoyed the company of Noah and Milcah every day, but to receive a visit from the older and younger sisters was an added treat.

"To what do we owe this honor?" he asked, smiling at Mahlah.

"You might know it is because we need your help once again." Mahlah returned the smile of genuine pleasure at seeing her cousin. There was no one she trusted more. *What a help and a rock he has been to us for years,* she thought.

"Well, you know that I am always willing to do what I can for you." He was looking from one familiar pretty face to the next. Milcah and Tirzah had grown to be almost as beautiful as their older sisters. In fact, some thought

Tirzah, who was now taller than any of them and carried herself in a regal manner, was the most beautiful of all.

"What is it that you need from me?" he asked.

"We want you to be overseer of all that we've inherited, Asriel," said Milcah. "We especially need you to oversee things when the pillar rises and we know Israel will start to move shortly. You know, Asriel, like our father did.

"You are familiar with all of it because you've been here helping us each time we have moved since I can remember." Milcah was exaggerating a little. She loved Asriel dearly and trusted him implicitly.

Tirzah nodded. "Yes Asriel, we need you and want to put things in your hands when we are moving. We love you and trust you. No one else fits what we need." She was smiling at him with eyes sparkling.

He felt himself blushing at such high praise. "And what have you to say about this, my dear Noah?" he asked light-heartedly.

Noah looked into his eyes. It was plain to see that this man loved her and would gladly give up his life to please her. *How dear a friend is my cousin. I praise Jehovah for providing us such a loyal helper.*

Noah wanted to hug him, but they had gone past the playful gestures as the years drew on. She respected how he felt for her and was careful not to flirt or tease as she had when they were children and before she had fallen in love with Malcham.

"Of course I agree with the others, Asriel. There is no on else who loves us and would see to our well being like you! You are like one of us. We can never thank you enough for all you've done for us already, but we need you as a man to do this for us."

"You are sure that I can handle it?" He had admitted to himself that he liked the idea. It would better fit his age and growing experience.

"You know almost as much about our father's business as he did," Mahlah assured him. Uncle Joseph has recommended that we ask you. He seems to have no doubt that you are capable of handling the position. He says the position is one of great responsibility and your salary should be increased accordingly."

Asriel was listening to Mahlah, but he was facing the pillar of cloud, which always stood in front of the camp. As Mahlah was speaking, he saw it begin to rise into the air. Time had come for Israel to continue their journeying.

"Look!" he told his cousins. "We're to move again! I'll try the overseer job this time and see if I want to continue when we find our next camping place."

The girls turned to look. It was truly an awesome sight. They never ceased to be filled with wonder at the glory and mystery of the cloud that guided Israel—the presence of their God.

We have a lot to do," Asriel reminded them. "I'll take care of the animals with Epher and Shechem and the other workers. Go back and get the women started on disassembling the tents. We'll be coming with the donkeys, oxen, and carts as quickly as we can.

Chapter 5

The pillar began to move. There was an unusual atmosphere of expectation and excitement throughout the camps. When the trumpet sounded for Manasseh to move out, Asriel had all Zelophehad's family, workers, animals, and possessions ready to go. The preparation went as smoothly as if Zelophehad had himself organized and supervised the move.

Each knew his or her part in the packing and loading, and each performed willingly and cheerfully under the overseeing of Asriel who worked as hard as anyone in the group. He instructed but he also helped in any way he was needed.

It became obvious that he was, indeed, the right man for this job. He informed the sisters he would be pleased to be their overseer if he could still be the chief shepherd when they were not moving. They readily agreed.

But Israel, for several months, was not to stay very long in one place. They were nearing their destination but there was still a lot to be accomplished before they entered the land God had given them on the west side of the Jordan River.

The pillar led them forward and the first camp they made was in Oboth, the next at the ruins of Abarim in the wilderness before Moab heading east. The next camp was in the valley of Zared, and when they moved again, they camped on the other side of the river of Arnon, which is in the wilderness of the country of the Amorites and of the Moabites. The country of their kinsmen, the Ammonites, was to the north and east. God had warned Moses not to enter the Ammonite's land or disturb them in any way because God had given them their land.

When Israel reached the place that is called Beer, God spoke to Moses and told him, ". . . Gather the people together and I will give them water." (Numbers 21:16 KJV)

None of the family or their near kin was present at this occasion, but the leaders of the tribe described it later. When the people had gathered, Moses pointed out a place where God had told him they should dig, and Moses instructed the leaders to dig and they dug with their staves. Instead of telling the laborers to dig, God had the leaders

digging. Before long, the water came forth in abundance.

They celebrated. Water was so dear in this dry and thirsty land. Someone made a song and they sang, "Spring up, O well; sing ye unto it: The princes digged the well, the nobles of the people digged it, by the direction of the lawgiver, with their staves . . ." (Numbers 21:17,18 KJV)

The pillar led on, from the wilderness to Mattanah, from there to Nahaliel, and from there to Bamoth in a valley in the country of Moab, to mount Pisgah where they could look toward Jeshimon.

From this place Moses sent messengers to Sihon, the king of the Amorites, asking permission to pass through the land—as he had asked Edom. The king would not listen and immediately began preparations for war; he readied his people and came out against Israel.

God told Moses that He would give this king, his people, and his cities and his land to Israel. He told them to go out and fight and possess it.

This time Asriel was not called upon to go to war, but his cousins, Helek and Abiezer, Joseph's two older sons, were sent. The fighting went on for weeks, with more men being called to help occupy cities from Aroer by Arnon, up to Gilead where God delivered the Amorites into Israel's hands as He had promised. He ordered the people destroyed, but the cattle and the spoil of the cities He permitted them to keep.

More men were called after the fighting was over. Sihon and his kingdom were destroyed, but there was the gruesome task of burying the dead—from both sides. There were, of course, many more dead of the Amorites, but Israel lost warriors, too—and among them was Malcham, the brave young Benjamite, Noah's love.

The pillar rose one day and led the rest of Israel up into the Amorite country to move into the splendid cities God had given them. The men of Reuben, Gad, and Manasseh were impressed with this land Israel had just taken. They could see it was a land particularly suited for the raising of cattle.

Israel's army turned and went up to Bashan, and Og, the king of Bashan, came out against them at Edrei. The army had been replenished as the rest of the people came on into the deserted cities and soldiers were freed to go back to their places in the advancing host.

God delivered threescore cities in all the region of Argob, in the kingdom of Og, the giant, in Bashan. Once again, there was the awful task of burying the dead and putting things back in order. It was hard work clearing the land of putrefying bodies, but it had to be done quickly to avoid spreading of disease that accompanies war and destruction.

When Helek and Abiezer later spoke of their army service, they said this was the worst part. The battles were quick and furious, but clearing the aftermath was tedious and filthy and sad.

The cloudy pillar, the glory of God, lifted once again and led them to the plains of Moab on the east side of Jordan by Jericho. This was recently Moabite country because the Amorites had pushed them off the land Israel had just conquered. Also the Midianites dwelt here.

Moab was filled with fear and dread when Israel's thousands of tents were pitched and settled there. They had witnessed what Jehovah could do. Balak, the king of the Moabites, and his people knew what Israel had done to the two Amorite kings. There was no longer one Amorite left to be seen and the Israelites now possessed and occupied their cities and countryside.

A well-known prophet called Balaam dwelt in the east of Balak's domain. This man had a reputation for mighty works. And when Balak summoned his officials to confer with him about the situation and danger the Isralites posed, they soon agreed their only hope was to call upon this prophet, Balaam, whom they believed served the God of Israel—Jehovah.

"If we can get Balaam to come and curse this people," Balak reasoned, "there is a chance we will not have to suffer the fate of Sihon and Og and their people."

They sent representatives—elders from the Midianites and Moabites—with offers of great rewards of divination to Balaam and he did not come. The frantic Balak sent more and honorable ambassadors to Balaam.

When this group returned, they were accompanied by the famous prophet. The king's heart lightened at the thought of this man's influence with the God of Israelites. *If he curses them,* he thought, t*hey will surely be cursed and we can, at least, chase them away from our land.*

He greeted the prophet royally. He listened to all his instructions and had altars built and sacrifices ready for the offering exactly as he was told.

Balaam wanted to curse Israel but every time he opened his mouth to do so, a blessing came out instead of the curse. Balak took him to a high place where he was able to see the tents of Israel in their camp that formed a giant cross. There they went through the whole process again; and once again there came out blessings instead of the curse they had hoped for.

Then Balak took him to the top of Peor. Their altars were built, sacrifices were offered, and Balaam tried this third time. He could speak nothing but blessings!

Balak was furious, but Balaam told him no matter what the king paid, he could only say what God allowed him to say. He even went into a trance and spoke of this Almighty One: "I shall see him, but not now: I shall behold him, but not nigh: there shall come a Star out of Jacob, and a Sceptre shall rise out of Israel, and shall smite the corners of Moab, and destroy all the children of Sheth." (Numbers 24:17 KJV)

What these people did not know was that Jehovah was a God like no other they had ever seen or heard of. He did not operate in the manner of the gods they knew, and these people, Israel, were His chosen people. He had chosen them not because they were especially good or handsome or lovable or intelligent, or braver in battle, but because it was His will.

Jehovah was The God among gods, the LORD of lords. He honored His promises.

Balaam could not curse the people, but he taught another way to corrupt them. He told Balak to socialize with the Israelites—to let especially the young people—boys and girls fraternize and become familiar with each other. "They will begin to find your ways more attractive and exciting—especially your religion—and it will draw them away from this Jehovah," he counseled.

Chapter 6

As Israel settled into this new place, things calmed to the point they tried to get into their routine again, but all the people realized it could not be the same, living so near the Moabites and the Midianites whose way of life was so different.

The daughters of Zelophehad had never been active in the social life in the camps because their father had kept them working and never encouraged visitors. Now they began to see new people among their neighbors—people their age and younger—visiting and playing with the Israelites.

These people looked and acted so different. They were mostly very attractive and when encountered around the camp, looked into one's eyes with a bold and almost impudent and arrogant stare as if asking a personal question.

The young men and women all seemed to be handsome and wore bright clothes that made the Israelite's way of dressing seem dull and uninteresting—especially the female dress. They were much less modest. Having them around, turning the heads of the Israelite men, was causing the young women of the camps to try to emulate some of their styles.

The young Israelite men could not keep from staring at these girls who always seemed to be laughing and teasing and making everyday life much more interesting and pleasing.

Malah and Tirzah saw quite a bit of what was happening around them. Noah and Milcah, who spent most of the daylight hours with the sheep, were exposed to very little of the change. The visiting Moabites and Midianites seldom ventured to places where work was being done.

One morning Noah and Milcah had been gone to tend the sheep for over two hours when visitors appeared at the tent.

Joseph and his younger daughter Lanodah arrived and were heartily welcomed by Mahlah and Tirzah. Joseph felt obligated to do what he could to help his nieces. There was something that was bothering him and he wanted to discuss it with Mahlah. His oldest daughter Everah had just been married. She was five or six years younger than Mahlah and two years younger than Noah. It had caused him to think about his nieces' situation and what might be done to see these girls married and fulfilling their duty to become wives and mothers in Israel.

After Mahlah had welcomed them with a cool drink and Tirzah had washed their feet, they settled down to talk.

"Mahlah, what was the young man's name who wanted to marry you and Zelophehad's refusal frightened everyone else away? What tribe was he from?"

Mahlah stopped smiling and looked down at her hands in her lap. "His name is Hezron and he is a Reubenite. He is the brother of Father's young wife, Metah."

"I thought they were Reubenites, but I wasn't sure. Have you heard from him, Mahlah? Does he know you're free to marry him now?"

"I have never heard from him since that night Father threw him out of our tent. I think at first it was because he feared if he upset Father again, it might endanger me. Uncle Joseph, you just don't know how angry and violent Father became when the subject of the marriage of his daughters was brought up!"

Joseph nodded his head. "Oh yes, I have heard from several sources, including my sons, how utterly irrational he was about it."

"But as time passed by," Mahlah continued, "I think maybe Hezron gave it up as impossible and decided to get on with his life. He is older than I, so he is far past the age where men are expected to start families and must have been having pressure applied long ago."

Joseph saw a tear fall onto his niece's graceful hands. She raised one of her hands to brush the tears away from her face. She looked up at him and smiled. "I get impatient with myself for crying. It doesn't help at all. I tell myself I must be practical."

Joseph nodded again. "The practical thing to do in this case is to send word to Hezron that your father is dead and that you are now free to marry."

"Oh, do you really think so after all these years?"

"If you really still care for him, Mahlah, it is the only thing that makes sense. I am sure that when word gets around that Zelophehad has died and you and your sisters are free to marry, there will soon be others who will be coming to ask for you." Joseph was happy to remind her of that. She seemed to consider herself not worthy of marriage. "For instance," he continued, "my sons think you are very beautiful. Everyone far and wide, knows what workers you and your sisters are. You are nowhere near past childbearing age! How could any sensible young man not consider you as a wife?

"So if you want Hezron, it makes sense to find out if he still wants you. If he doesn't, you need to be ready to consider other proposals which I know will be coming." He finished this practical summation of her circumstances with a big smile—pleased to be informing her of what he considered a very happy situation for her.

Mahlah was smiling again. "Uncle Joseph, thank you for telling me what you think I should do. Did you know Father gave his blessing for my marriage to Hezron and Noah's to Malcham the night he died?"

Joseph was surprised. "No, I didn't know that. I thought he was very angry."

"His anger was at Hasenuah and himself and it completely changed his attitude toward us."

Tirzah's face was beaming at the memory of that one happy evening with her father. "Uncle Joseph, he told us that he loved us and that he was proud of us and that we were good and beautiful daughters. He thanked us and told us he was sorry for the way he treated us."

Now it was Joseph who had to wipe away tears. "My dear nieces, I am so happy for you. Zelophehad was not a bad person. His situation just grew to be too much for him to bear, I guess."

Mahlah reached and patted Joseph's hand. "You must not think that he died with anger at you, Uncle. He loved you and respected you. He told us to get you to help us.

"Yes, Uncle," Tirzah added, "he said you were a good man and would deal honestly and truthfully with us."

"I am so thankful that you've told me these things, girls. It is a relief to know he didn't blame me for the death of his son." He bowed his head trying to collect himself. "The whole thing is just so sad," he whispered.

Mahlah waited a moment and then announced, "I think I will go and tell Hezron that I am free! I would be very pleased if you could go with me, Uncle Joseph. Could you?"

"I'd be honored," he told her, "it's the least I can do." He stood up and for the first time since Zelophehad's and Hasenuah's deaths he stood straight. A terrible burden had kept him bent like an old man. Now it was gone.

"And after we get your situation cleared up, I will go see Noah's young man!"

Mahlah smiled happily at him and Tirzah hugged him and kissed him on the cheek. "You are a good man, just like Father told us!"

117

Mahlah and Joseph walked outside, discussing plans for the trip to see Hezron, the Reubenite. Tirzah turned back to her cousin, Lanodah. "Isn't this all wonderful?" she asked.

"Yes," her cousin answered, "I am so happy you are all going to be able to live normal lives now! My brothers say you are rich, and any one can see how pretty you are. You are going to have men by the dozens come courting you!"

She giggled. "But Tirzah, are you and the others going to join in visiting and socializing now? You have kept to yourselves too much. People need to see you and get to know you."

Tirzah shook her head. "I'm satisfied with the way we live now. We seem to always have plenty to do."

"No, Tirzah—that's what I mean. You stay too close to home. You need to get out." Lanodah just couldn't understand such an attitude.

"I don't know about that," Tirzah laughed.

"I know, cousin, what you need is to come along with me and Everah and her new husband to the feast the Midianites are having tomorrow."

"Are those the people we have been seeing in the camp?"

"Yes," said Lanodah enthusiastically. "They are so friendly and a lot of fun." She grinned, "I do think the young men are so handsome and the girls' clothes are so attractive!"

"Does your father know you are socializing with them? They seem so . . . uh—so bold—or something." Tirzah couldn't come up with the right word.

Lanodah laughed again. "Father is one of the leaders of our tribe and these people invited him and his family especially to this feast along with the other leaders. If your father were still alive it would have been him and his family.

"I don't think father will go—but we are! Just everyone will be going."

Tirzah felt vaguely disturbed. "No, Lanodah, I don't think I'd feel right going to their feast. It is to honor their god isn't it? Lanodah, you need to be careful. Jehovah is our God. Will your brothers be going?"

"No, I don't think so—all they ever think of is work, work, work. But I'd bet they'd be tripping all over themselves if they got to know some of these Midianite girls!"

Tirzah was searching for more words to caution her cousin further when Joseph put his head in the tent door and said, "Daughter, it's time to go."

118

Chapter 7

Joseph and Mahlah set the date for their trip into the camp of Reuben a week from the day Mahlah decided she should go. They also decided that Tirzah should go with them.

Mahlah arranged for Levah and her two young sons to stay in the big tent while they were gone to keep an eye on all the belongings. The older son, Assir, was big enough to have begun training to help Ishi, his father, with the animals. But for the time that Mahlah and Tirzah would be gone, Assir was to stay at the tent "to guard our things," and Tirzah said it in a manner that would convince him it was a position worthy of his age and experience.

It had worked and Assir and Jahath proudly accepted their assignments as security guards. Mahlah had told Noah that as soon as they had contacted Hezron and that matter was settled one way or the other, she would send Tirzah to take the shepherdess' place. This would allow Uncle Joseph to accompany her to the Benjamite camp to let Malcham know she was now free to marry.

Neither girl would allow her hopes to obscure the fact that these men might not have waited all the years that had passed. But they could not keep from hoping. They had experienced so little happiness in life that the bright memory of a brave and strong young man's love was a tremendous thing—a wonderful and shining reality amid the darkness they had endured for years.

Each had, at times, thought it must have been a dream. *It couldn't have happened to someone like me.* But the truth that it had actually happened was there. It had happened and she clung to it with great thankfulness and joy in her heart. And now, the time had come to deal with it. Their hearts beat overtime with the excitement as they "came to life" once again. *I might soon be married to the man I love! I might still be the mother of sons and daughters of Israel.*

Milcah and Tirzah were happy for their older sisters. The things they had heard their uncle say had started them thinking of marriage and a family. It was so strange to think of such things. These things had just never occurred to them the way they had grown up. But they were now nearing the age when girls in Israel were considered for betrothal. How different their life was becoming.

On the morning she had set, Mahlah and Tirzah were prepared to go. They had finished gathering manna and were waiting when Joseph appeared. He was tall and straight and handsome once again. They thought how remarkably like their father he looked now except for the pleasant look on his face. *Poor father, always so unhappy.*

"All ready?" Joseph asked.

"Yes, we are more than ready; we are eager to get started," Tirzah said.

Joseph laughed. *This Tirzah was a pleasure to be with. She just seemed to love everyone.* "Very well. Girls, I'm going to let you set the pace. We'll go at your speed. I plan to travel all day with three rest stops of about an hour each and then we will sleep wherever we are when it nears sundown. Two days will most likely get us to Reuben's camp."

He looked to each girl. They both agreed it was a good plan. He pointed out the direction and Mahlah led off on the journey that could decide what her life would be.

Joseph was surprised at the pace and stamina of his companions. They kept a pace close to what he would have walked had he been alone. He called the rest stops and the girls were ready to start again when he said it was time. All three were weary when they stopped for the night.

They talked very little, ate some manna and drank from their water bottles, rolled in their cloaks, and went to sleep immediately. Mahlah woke early and roused the others. They gathered more manna, ate and were on their way. By early afternoon they were into the Reubenite camp. Joseph asked some men standing outside a tent for directions to Beerah's tent. He came back to report to Mahlah and Tirzah they were very close.

He suggested the girls might want to wash the dust from their faces before meeting Beerah and his family. All three dampened cloths and washed the best they could. The girls held a small mirror for each other and helped with getting hair combed and suitably arranged. Joseph watched the process noting how little it took to make a real beauty ready for an important meeting. The more time he spent with these girls, the more he loved and respected them. It was as if God had given him four more daughters.

He looked at Mahlah. Her face was glowing with excitement; her dark eyes were bright and sparkling. Her voice had a bit of a tremor. Oh, how he hoped Hezron had waited for her. She deserved something good. He thought he saw her hands shaking as she was helping Tirzah with her hair. But she remained calm and capable as always.

When they reached Beerah's tent (it was unmistakable—the largest and the richest) the girls stood back and Joseph went near the door.

"Ho, Beerah!" he called and waited. Beerah came to the door of the tent and took a step backward when Joseph stepped up to greet him. Joseph smiled at him and said, "I am Joseph of Manasseh, Beerah. I have come on an urgent errand."

Beerah stared at him a moment and then stepped toward him. "I thought you were Zelophehad! You look very much like him." Then he greeted him with the customary embrace. "Come into my tent. You are welcome," he said.

Joseph turned to the waiting girls and motioned them to step up. "These are my nieces, Mahlah and Tirzah." They came to Joseph.

Beerah smiled with happy recognition. "I remember you and your gracious hospitality!" Mahlah and then Tirzah each offered her hand and made a slight bow of respect.

"Come in! Come in! I want my wife to meet you. She never could believe all the good things we told her about you and your sisters."

He led the way into the pleasant sitting area and saw them seated. He motioned for the servant girls to wash their feet and bring them water. "Iloriah!" he called to the back of the tent. "Come! We have guests."

His wife emerged from a curtained back room. She was smiling until she saw Mahlah. She knew instantly who this beautiful woman was and feared it meant trouble for her family.

Beerah went to her side and put his arm around her shoulder to bring her to their guests, who stood to greet her with respect. "Iloriah, this is Mahlah and Tirzah, Zelophehad's daughters and this is Joseph, his brother."

Mahlah's heart sank when she saw the look on Iloriah's face. *What did it mean?* She and Tirzah made their little bows of respect.

Iloriah spoke to Joseph, "Welcome to our home. Excuse my hesitation. You look so much like your brother!"

Joseph nodded. "A lot of people tell me that. There was only a little over a year's difference in our ages." He too had seen the look on Iloriah's face and decided it did not bode well for their visit's purpose.

Then Iloriah quietly spoke to Mahlah and Tirzah. "I must thank you for your kindness to my daughter Metah while she was with you. She is very grateful for the way you and your sisters accepted her and treated her while she was there."

"Is she here?" Mahlah asked politely.

"No. Metah has been married for three years. She has even given us a grandson," Beerah answered for Iloriah who could not make herself stop looking at Mahlah.

"I'm very happy for her." Mahlah spoke sincerely and Tirzah nodded her head enthusiastically.

Joseph was watching Mahlah and hoping to end the formalities and get to the question they wanted to ask.

Beerah caught the look of impatience that fleetingly appeared on Joseph's face. He led his wife to a divan and they sat down and motioned for his guests to sit again. He looked at Mahlah and said, "I know you did not come all this way just to enjoy a polite visit." He turned to Joseph and said, "Would you like to tell us why you came?"

"Yes, thank you!" Joseph was grateful for the understanding this Reubenite was showing. "My brother, Zelophehad, died five months ago from the bite of a fiery serpent," he began.

Iloriah gave a little gasp and Beerah bent forward. Joseph had their attention. "My brother begged Mahlah's forgiveness for his actions toward your son. As he was dying, he told her he would bless their union if it were still possible. Mahlah didn't think coming here was the right thing to do since it has been years since she heard from Hezron. But I knew she loved him and still loves him with all her heart, so I convinced her that she should at least come and see what his situation is."

Iloriah was silently weeping. "Hezron loved you so much." She spoke to Mahlah. "He was so broken and unhappy for so long!"

Beerah had a stricken look on his face. "Mahlah, we finally convinced him it was best for him to marry and begin a family. He still loved you but we knew there was no hope; we thought it was his duty to get on with his life. He is my oldest son, you know."

Tirzah stood and went to her sister to put a comforting arm around her.

"Hezron has been married two years and has a little son," Beerah finished.

Mahlah got to her feet. "Thank you for receiving us. I know my father caused you a lot of grief," she told her hosts as they also stood. "You've told us what we needed to know and now we shouldn't trouble you any further. You have a wonderful son. I am honored to have been loved by him and asked to be his wife."

Mahlah was turning to leave the tent but Beerah stepped close to her and put his hand on her shoulder. "Wait!" he cried. "Mahlah, you can't go. I know my son still loves you and he would never forgive us if we let you go without at least seeing him!"

"No, please, no." Mahlah kept walking toward the light coming in the tent door. I don't think I can take it. It hurts too much already. It would only stir up his hurt again."

She turned to Iloriah, "Just tell him I am happy for him that he has a son."

A figure appeared at the door and although it was silhouetted, she knew it was Hezron. She felt trapped. Now she would have to bring back all his hurt. She wished she had left the moment they said he was married.

"Mahlah! Is it really you?"

"Yes, Hezron. Here I am after all these years—just a little late. How are you?" She tried to sound cheerful.

"I am so happy to see you! I can't believe this is happening." He was looking down into the lovely face that had stayed with him all the years of separation.

He could see tears welling up in her eyes. "Your parents have told us about your marriage and your little son." A tear escaped and ran down the beautiful face he had thought he would never see again.

She ducked her head to wipe the tear and tried to walk by him.

"Mahlah, you can't go!" He took her arm. "We have to talk about this. My sister told me that she heard your uncle say that Zelophehad is dead." He guided her to the door. "We have to talk about this. I don't want to lose you again."

He looked back to his parents and Joseph and Tirzah. "Please wait for us for a little while," he asked earnestly. "I have to talk to Mahlah alone."

With that, they disappeared, Hezron guiding Mahlah to a place between several tents, where they could sit and talk.

Beerah and his wife led Tirzah and Joseph back to the sitting area and they all made an effort at conversation. They ended up discussing the growing presence of the Midianites among the people and how many of their leaders had attended these people's religious rituals.

Beerah said he had heard from men who had been there, the unspeakable things these people did in the worship of their god Baal-peor. Iloriah blushed and nudged him with her elbow—nodding toward the young visitor. Tirzah realized that she had been right in trying to warn Lanodah there might be something wrong with these people.

Joseph was taken by surprise. "I had no idea," he said. I let my daughters go to one of their feasts the other night."

Then came the discussion of how the young people were being influenced by their parents' acceptance of these people who worshipped another god. They all agreed that the ones most affected were middle-aged men—especially influential men—men in leadership positions in Israel.

Mahlah returned to the tent in about a half hour. Her attitude seemed to have changed completely from when Hezron had led her away. She seemed calm and composed.

"Didn't Hezron come back with you?" Iloriah asked.

"Yes, he guided me back, but he has gone to his tent," Mahlah answered. "I hope our visit hasn't upset you." She turned to Joseph. "We should be leaving now, shouldn't we?"

He was relieved to see she was taking it all so well. He reached out a hand to Iloriah and said, "Thank you for your hospitality. I am very pleased to have met you both."

Tirzah made another little bow to Iloriah and Beerah and then followed Mahlah out into the bright afternoon.

Iloriah said to Beerah, "You were right about this Mahlah. I know Hezron asked her again to marry him and I think she has refused so as not to upset his life all over again. She is an extraordinary woman."

On the walk back to Manasseh, Mahlah seemed thoughtful but not particularly sad. She told Joseph and Tirzah that Hezron had asked her again to be his wife and she thought it best not to accept.

When they arrived home she thanked Joseph for his part in getting the matter of Hezron settled. "Now I can get back to reality and get on with the rest of my life. It was a beautiful thing but so fragile and fleeting. I still can't believe it really happened to me.

But when Hezron told me he wanted to marry me, I thought of my parents and what a second wife means and I just couldn't disrupt so many lives by becoming a second wife.

Chapter 8

Now it was Noah's turn. The first time she and Mahlah had a chance to talk she insisted that Mahlah tell her all about the visit to the Reubenite camp and what had been her reasoning in refusing to marry Hezron.

"Noah," Mahlah began, "from the moment I saw his mother's face I knew, whatever the situation, that marrying him would upset all of their lives. When I found that he already had a son who would be his lawful heir, my heart told me there would be tension over that if I should be able to give him sons. Neither of his parents even hinted that he loved his wife—or, for that matter, that she loved him. It had all been a matter of doing what is expected of you and getting on with life

But all of us knew that it wasn't that way with Hezron and me; it was more like our mother and father. So I knew that one day his wife would really come to resent me. And who knows what kind of trouble that would bring?

"I love him, Noah; I don't want to cause him unhappiness for the rest of his life."

Noah completely understood, having lived with a miserable mother and a tormented father for years. "Did you tell this to Hezron?"

"I told him some of it from a woman's perspective."

"What did he say when he talked with you?" Noah was thinking about what may lie ahead of her if she found Malcham again.

"Noah, he was so happy to see me! He told me he had not tried to communicate with me for fear Father might harm me. Father was a raving mad man when he ordered him out!

"Hezron said he loved me still and seeing me again made him feel as if we had never been separated. He said his wife was much younger than I and had been like his sister, Metah, when she married Father. She loved the idea of marrying a rich, influential man rather than the man himself. She knew all about me and it didn't seem to matter that she was marrying a man who loved someone else."

"I can't understand an attitude like that, can you, Mahlah?"

Her sister shook her head. "Never," she said, "but that's the way a lot of people reason. And Noah, it works out very well many times. I don't think Hezron is miserable. He appeared to be doing very well.

"It was when he spoke to me about his little son that it was impressed upon me that I should leave him as he is. I just suddenly realized that our marriage was not meant to be." Mahlah gave a little ironic laugh. "It was such a lovely, lovely thing we had the short time it lasted, but our marriage was just not meant to be," she repeated. "I am most certainly not happy, but I have an unexplainable peace about it, Noah. I know I did the right thing."

She hugged her shepherdess sister. "I hope your visit will be different, Noah."

A date was then set for the visit to the Benjamite camp. It had been planned that Tirzah would take Noah's place with the sheep, but Noah decided she wanted Milcah to come along with her, so Asriel arranged for Jahdiel and Eliel to help him instead and little Assir got to go help his father, Ishi—doing "a real man's" work.

This journey was longer than Mahlah's but Noah and Milcah had endurance to spare. Joseph found there was no need to make allowances for them. They kept pace.

He thought Noah was more beautiful than ever. She seemed to glow with anticipation of meeting again the only man who had ever really captured her attention. Joseph looked at her and remembered the stories of her indifference to all the young men who sought after her.

His sons had told him she was friendly and flirty, and happy to be around them, but had no particular interest in any of the young men even before she met Malcham.

The news that Mahlah had found her love married had sobered Noah's thinking somewhat, but Noah still hoped that Malcham had waited for her. It had been a long while since she had heard from him, but she truly believed she'd find he had waited.

It took two whole days and part of a third to reach Benjamin. Along the way they saw many instances of the fraternizing at every age level among their people with the Midianites. Joseph sensed that more and more of his Israelite brothers were assuming the ways of the outsiders who had no respect for them and openly despised their God, Jehovah. He couldn't understand why the leaders were going along with it. He knew trouble was upon them.

He had ordered his sons and daughters to refuse any more invitations to their celebrations. He had tried to tell his friends and the other men of influence he knew that these people were against the God who had brought them out of Egypt and had given them all they owned and was leading them to their new land.

Most of them thought he was being too particular and could see nothing wrong with being friends with the Midianites. Some of the men became downright angry with him and turned away. Joseph was beginning to see that something would have to be done soon or these Baal-peor followers would take over.

Noah and Milcah were shocked at the change in the atmosphere in the camps. They had spent all their time out with the sheep and had been unaware these things had become so prevalent so quickly.

Somehow, upon reaching the Benjamite part of Israel, Joseph took a wrong turn and instead of entering the residential area, the travelers found themselves in the place where the Benjamites did their business.

Over the years of journeying, these places had developed as the normal result of the needs of the people. Within the camp of each tribe—usually at a central location—a little traveling business district had evolved. It was a place to have equipment repaired, replace worn-out tent coverings, buy and sell animals, and so on. It was also a place to hire workers and make marriage arrangements, or just to meet and visit with friends, and possibly talk with a leader or a judge.

This was a place women did not frequent unless it was to find help in an emergency. Women produced items to be sold or traded here, but they did not stay. They left it up to the men to do the selling or the bartering of their goods.

Joseph was into the place before he realized it and stopped to find someone to direct him. "I'm sorry, girls," he said, "just stay close to me and I'll get you out of here as quickly as I can."

The area seemed to be extremely busy, with men sitting in open booths displaying their wares and tents all around with men standing outside talking. There were little wooden benches set here and there where men could sit and exchange stories and opinions. Every bench was occupied and men were standing all around.

The travelers kept walking and suddenly came upon a large tent from which sounds of laughter and reveling could be heard. The tent was different looking, dyed bright colors with long thin little banners fluttering from the poles that supported it.

127

Men that were standing outside it looked at Joseph's companions and began to laugh and motion to them. Noah turned to Milcah as she drew up her veil over her head. "Cover your face, Milcah! Let's get away from here."

Joseph was horrified. He steered the girls in another direction. He wanted to go back and confront the offenders but he reasoned that would be a mistake. He had to get the girls away.

Noah was wishing she had brought her sling. Milcah was indignant. They bumped

into two Midianite girls in their bright and attractive clothing heading toward the tent. The women were laughing and asked Joseph, "Don't you want to come along and join the fun?"

Then they heard someone call, "Zelophehad! This way!"

Joseph turned to see Abdon with two younger men hurrying toward them. He and the girls turned to them and were led out of the busy market place. Abdon stopped when they were well away from the hubbub and started to say something to Joseph. Then, taking a closer look, said, "But you are not Zelophehad!"

Joseph grabbed his hand and said, "No. I'm not, but I'm thankful for what you've done for us. I'm Joseph, Zelophehad's brother. I met you at the war games in Manasseh several years ago, Abdon."

Noah and Milcah were uncovering their faces and smiling at their rescuers.

The young men were delighted to see the faces of the ones they had rescued.

"Noah!" Abdon cried. "And is this you, Milcah? You are even prettier than I thought you would be!" To everyone's surprise she stood on tiptoe and kissed his cheek. He was such a kind man; she remembered how happy and secure he had made her and Tirzah feel when they were lonely and afraid. He introduced the young men as his nephews and Joseph thanked them profusely for their escort.

The girls smiled and made their little bows of respect. The nephews were dazzled and blushing. These were the daughters of Zelophehad they had heard so much about! They had been present at the celebration after the games when Zelophehad had made his outburst.

Joseph had collected himself enough to remember their purpose in coming. "Abdon, we are here to talk to Malcham," he began.

Abdon had started to open his mouth but decided to wait until Joseph finished.

Joseph went on, "Zelophehad died about five months ago from the bite of a fiery serpent. Before he died, he asked Noah to forgive him and blessed her union with Malcham if it were still possible. Noah has never given up loving

Malcham. We have come all this way to see if he still wants to marry her or if he has already married someone else."

Abdon bowed his head. Then he reached for Noah and embraced her saying, "God bless you for being faithful to my son! He loved you unwaveringly and never gave up hope that you would eventually be his wife. But that's no longer possible, Noah. Malcham was killed in the fighting with Sihon. We never even got to bury him. He lies somewhere in that Amorite land."

He was weeping now and both Noah and Milcah put their arms around him. The young men were silent. Joseph's heart filled with sympathy for this man who had lost a brave and good son. He brushed tears from his own eyes.

Noah released her hold on Abdon and sank to her knees in the dust crying out, "Oh my Malcham! How I do love you!" Noah bent her head to the ground, her shoulders shaking with the sobs. She felt as if someone were crushing her heart, a mighty weight upon her chest. *Oh! I am not* able *to bear this!*

Of all the eventualities she had considered regarding she and Malcham, the one thing that had never entered her mind was death. *He was so strong and full of life!*

Milcah knelt in the dust and put her arm around the broken Noah. "I'm so sorry Noah—so sorry." Milcah cried, too. It tore at her heart to see her sister suffering so. Noah had always been the light-hearted and laughing one of the five—telling them outlandish stories to keep them entertained—always finding humor in everyday happenings when their spirits were down. It was so sad to see that happy spirit completely trampled into the dust of the camp of Benjamin.

The young men, watching this beautiful young woman who had so loved their cousin and friend, struggled to keep from choking up and crying, too. Abdon stood remembering the night he sat with her two young sisters while Malcham visited with Noah. *They had so little time together.*

Joseph stood thinking how close Noah had come to real happiness after all the years of waiting only to have it taken away once again. He waited for Noah to finish with her crying.

"Oh my dear Malcham," she whispered this time. "Oh God—Jehovah God—help me to bear this. I can't bear this alone!" After a few more moments she lifted her head from the dust and rocks and started to rise. Milcah helped her to her feet.

"Uncle Joseph," she asked, "let us go home now."

He came to her and took her hand. "My dearest girl, I am so sorry it turned out this way."

She finally stood straight, wiping away tears and dirt with her veil, speaking softly with finality, "It is just as Mahlah said. It just wasn't meant to be."

Joseph turned to Abdon. "I am so sorry for your loss. Your son was a fine warrior and a fine young man." Abdon nodded his head still trying to control his tears.

"We will go on now," Joseph told him. "Thank you once again for getting us out of that mess. I never thought I'd see such a thing in the camps of Israel."

Abdon found his voice. "I am thankful we were there for you! But I can't let you go without having my wife meet the girl who meant so much to our son." He turned to Noah. "Dear Noah, can you find enough strength to come and meet Malcham's mother?"

Noah told him quietly, "I think Malcham would want me to, but will that not stir up her pain of the loss again? I can't promise I won't be crying."

Abdon considered for a moment. "I think you are right. Malcham loved you and he loved her. It is probably what he would want you to do. Even if it hurts I know Voldah would want to meet the only girl who won Malcham's love."

He took the grieving girl's arm and led her to his tent, which was quite a distance from the central area of Benjamin.

Abdon was so glad he had asked Noah to come to see his wife. The two talked and wept together. Milcah and the men saw it was a process that would help heal them both—so left them together and waited outside. The young nephews said goodbye and left for their home.

Things were much quieter in Abdon's neighborhood, but twice, as they were waiting for Noah, young men passed by with laughing and teasing Moabite women clinging to their arms and looking up into their faces.

Abdon said to Joseph, "We are most certainly due judgment from the LORD for allowing this to come about in Israel."

Joseph nodded his solemn agreement. "But how do we stop it? Our leaders are the ones encouraging it and going to their celebrations for their god Baal-peor. I keep trying to tell them that we're turning our young ones away from the true God, but I'm finding myself more and more in the minority as each day goes by. It is happening so quickly. It frightens me. I fear for our children!"

After awhile Noah and Voldah came out to invite them to eat and rest before starting home.

Chapter 9

Israel abode in Shittim and because of this, Zelophehad's daughters' lives were changing. Asriel and Joseph advised strongly that Noah and Milcah give up their shepherding because of the continuing presence of the Midianites about the camps. The girls could well afford to hire two shepherds to take their places. But Noah found it strange to stay around the tent. She longed for the solitude shepherds are sometimes afforded, but she also realized that having her sisters nearby to grieve with her was a blessing from Jehovah.

Asriel made sure their tent was positioned in the midst of tents with men so help would be quickly available if something were to happen. The girls did not go out one, or even two at a time. They made a rule that three together at a minimum would be allowed to venture away from the tent. Not that they even wanted to leave the tent, but life made it necessary now and then.

They visited with Lanodah and Everah on rare occasions, but their cousins were changing, trying to be more like the Midianite women. As Everah told them, "Those people really know how to enjoy life!" Joseph was not able to keep them under control all of the time. Everah's husband was of very little help. The death of their mother with the revelation of her murder of the baby, Oni, had an effect on them that would never be overcome.

The only other women the daughters of Zelophehad saw regularly were their hired man's wife, Levah, and Ahita, the sister of Jahdiel and Eliel who also worked for them.

More and more people of Israel were turning to the worship of the god Baal-peor. There was an element of distrust and division among neighbors. One didn't know whether the other was a faithful follower of Jehovah or had turned to the Midianite ways. The problem grew and magnified daily.

Early one morning Joseph woke to a sound he thought came from inside his tent. He rose and checked on Lanodah and his young sons. All seemed well but he was unable to see into all the corners and between furniture.

He returned to his sleeping area and lay down, still watching and listening. The sun was beginning to come up over the horizon and as he stared toward the curtain that separated his and Hasenuah's space from the front of the tent, he saw a figure rise from between some of the reed packing crates that doubled as seats and tables when Israel was not on the move.

The figure started toward his sleeping mat, then hesitated, and went back toward the front of the tent. He saw a little glint of light flash upon something the intruder held in his hand. Joseph reached for one of the paddles that lay against the side of the tent. His hand touched it and he secured his hold on it and swung it at the figure that was moving toward the tent door.

He missed! He lunged forward to tackle the person, crying out at the same instant to warn his children. Joseph and the intruder rolled together on the rug covering the dirt floor. The intruder had dropped his weapon and was trying now only to escape.

The boys and Lanodah appeared from their sleeping quarters and were looking in the growing light for an opening to jump in and help their father. One of the boys had picked up the paddle and swung it now, managing to strike the intruder a glancing blow to the head.

The intruder rolled away onto his back, his cloak falling away to reveal his face. It was not the face of a man, but of a young woman. She lay with her eyes closed, mouth open, bleeding from a scalp wound.

Joseph sat up and peered into the familiar countenance.

"It's Hoglah!" screamed Lanodah. "I think you killed her!" she cried.

"It is!" Joseph agreed. "Why on earth would she want to come into our tent?" His eyes caught sight of the weapon she had dropped. It was a long dagger that had flown across the tent when he had tackled her. "And with a knife!"

His son threw the paddle from him. "I'm sorry! I wouldn't have hurt Hoglah if I had known!" He was almost in tears, staring at all the blood.

Joseph stood up. "She's not dead," he reassured the would-be slayer. "Get a cloth and some water. I need something I can tear into strips for a bandage," he told Lanodah.

Lanodah brought him a cloth and Joseph quickly tore some of it into bandages. Then he took a piece and poured water on it and began to bathe Hoglah's face. He blotted the blood over the cut, which turned out to be very small and shallow and just above the right temple.

Joseph had washed most of the blood away and was holding a folded piece of cloth over the cut while wrapping a strip around her head when Hoglah opened her eyes. "Where is Aunt Hasenuah?" she demanded of the startled Joseph while trying to raise herself from the floor. Her uncle pushed her back.

Finishing the wrap, he split the end and fastened the bandage so the pressure would help stop the bleeding.

It came to him now why Hoglah had run away and what she was doing here in his tent with the knife and demanding to know the whereabouts of his wife.

"Hasenuah is dead, Hoglah; she died from a fiery serpent bite about seven months ago." He did not want to discuss it in the hearing of his children. "Let us get you to feeling a little stronger and I will take you to your sisters. You stay here and we will go gather manna and come back. We will eat and after that you should be able to walk the distance to their tent."

Hoglah lay with her eyes closed, waiting for her uncle and cousins to return. Suddenly she began to shake. Then she began to cry. Relief flooded her consciousness! She prayed and thanked Jehovah that He had done His work and she would not have to carry through on what she had determined and sworn to do the day she first heard of "the Revenger of Blood"—about a week before.

When her relatives returned with the manna, she was sitting up. The bleeding had stopped when Joseph had applied the pressure bandage and she felt no ill effects from the glancing blow of the paddle. What she felt most was profound relief from the lightening of a burden she had carried all these years—and she was very hungry.

Lanodah and Joseph dished up the manna for all five of them and poured milk. As they were eating, the boys kept their eyes on Hoglah. She managed to grin a reassuring grin at each of them and received a look of relief from each in return.

Once Lanodah started to ask a question, but her father shook his head at her and said, "We need to get the boys off to their work and then see Hoglah to her sisters as soon as possible."

When the boys left, Joseph came to Hoglah and asked, "Do you think you are strong enough to walk? It is quite a way, but we can stop and rest along the way if you need to."

Hoglah stood and walked around the tent. "I think I am all right, Uncle Joseph."

Joseph turned to Lanodah. "Do you want to come along? I don't like leaving you alone, what with all the strangers in our camp these days."

"Just let me get my new veil and I'm ready, Father."

Joseph took Hoglah's arm and started for the door. "Is the part of the camp where you've been staying filled with strangers and people turning away from our God?"

Hoglah shuddered. "Uncle, I can't understand how all this happened so fast. My mother and father are so upset and worried about what's going to happen. My father says God will judge us!" She paused and a look of realization and concern came over her face.

"They are going to be sick with worry about me! I'll have to get word back to them as soon as possible that I am all right. I left without telling them I was going."

Lanodah came out the door and took Hoglah's other arm and they were off. They covered the distance in about thirty minutes. Joseph stopped once to have Hoglah rest, but she protested she didn't need it. Suddenly, old memories were flooding her mind and she was more and more anxious to see her sisters. She dreaded seeing her father.

Mahlah came to the door when they called out and at first did not recognize the young girl between her uncle and her cousin.

"Mahlah," Hoglah cried out, "it's Hoglah. I've come home."

Mahlah's knees went weak and she almost stumbled. Noah, Milcah, and Tirzah were right behind her to catch her. They all stood staring in unbelief. "Hoglah, we thought you were dead!" Noah blurted out.

"What happened to you?" Tirzah wanted to know—noticing the bandage.

Milcah went to her sister and hugged her. "Yes, what happened, Hoglah?"

"I'll tell you all about it—just take us into the tent and let me sit down," Hoglah said to the astonished girls.

"Oh, do come in," Mahlah told the three visitors. "I am just so surprised, I've forgotten everything." They trooped inside and Mahlah and Tirzah found seats for all.

Joseph thought they were about to begin the foot washing welcome ritual and said, "Don't bother with the formal welcome. We would like some water to drink but then we must talk. There are things we must tell Hoglah and there are things she must tell us."

All the girls nodded. Mahlah poured water and Tirzah handed cups to Hoglah, Lanodah, and Joseph. Then they took their seats and all eyes turned to Joseph who was looking very serious.

"I think we should let Hoglah begin. Do you know that she came into my tent during the night with the intent of killing Hasenuah?"

Hoglah's sisters were even more astonished at this question and now all eyes were on her. She looked at Joseph and then into her sisters' eyes each in turn. She included Lanodah. Then she said deliberately, "It's true, if Hasenuah had been alive and asleep on her mat beside Uncle Joseph, she would be dead now! I swore to myself a week ago that I would do it or die in the effort."

They stared at her. They could see there was no doubt she meant it. She had made the statement with a cold emphasis that frightened them.

"Why on earth would you want to do that?" Mahlah asked, but they all had already guessed.

"Because I saw her cruelly stab our baby brother with the arrow the Amalekites dropped when someone frightened them away!"

"You saw it and that's why you ran away," said Noah.

"I saw it, but I didn't know if Hasenuah saw me. After I brought the women to help Mother that day I stayed until the baby was born. Then I came to tell you the good news. A little later I went back because I saw the women who had attended her going to check on their families. I kept thinking I should go to her—and finally I did.

"When it happened, I didn't know what to do. I knew if Hasenuah could kill that sweet little innocent baby, she was certainly capable of killing me. I didn't know where to turn. My mother lay dead—my father cared nothing for me. Hasenuah was my most trusted relative apart from them! I was a terrified eleven-year-old, so I did nothing.

But the day we were moving out and Hasenuah kept looking at me and asking me questions, I was sure she had seen me when she killed our brother and she was coming to kill me that evening. So I ran away."

"Poor little girl," Noah said and went to sit beside Hoglah and put an arm around her. "You almost told me one day didn't you?"

"Yes, I almost told," admitted Hoglah, "but I was glad that Father interrupted because I thought if I told any one, that person might be in danger too."

All three of the other sisters went to Hoglah and kissed her and welcomed her home.

"Now we'll all be mother, father, and brother to each other," Tirzah decided.

After a time, Hoglah continued her account of how she traveled alone and had found a new family. "I prayed and prayed and I just know that God took care of me and put me in a safe and happy home where I had everything I needed to heal and comfort me."

Hoglah told them about her six brothers and that she was the long-awaited and prayed-for daughter of a happy and secure Reubenite woman called Anthah, and the daughter of the most caring father any girl could ask for—a Reubenite named Reuben!

As she talked about her new parents, all her sisters laughed with happiness for her.

Milcah told her, "Here we thought you were dead and all that time you were enjoying the life we could only dream of."

Hoglah's face clouded over. "I must get word back to them that I am safe. The only time they asked where I came from, I told them I was the daughter of a rich and influential man. I know they thought I was making it all up, but they never to this day asked me again.

"They will be frantic, with all the Midianites making themselves part of Israel and our people worshipping their awful god and taking on their ways—I must let my family know I'm safe."

Joseph and Lanodah had listened to the account of Hoglah's exile and watched the happy reunion. They both felt guilt because they had loved the one who had brought about all the grief and sorrow this group of girls had gone through.

But Joseph spoke now. "Hoglah, you haven't asked and we haven't told you about your father."

Hoglah had not warmed to Joseph as the other girls had. She, of course, had no way of knowing that he had brought Hasenuah to confess to Zelophehad and to the girls when he found out what she had done and, consequently, he had everything in his power to help them and was still helping them.

She looked at him with a frown and said, "No, I haven't; do you want to tell me now?"

Joseph caught the sarcastic edge in her voice and the little note of defiance in her speech. Considering what she had seen and what she had endured, he decided she had a right to feel as she did.

"I wouldn't say I want to tell you, Hoglah, but you need to know. Your father died several months ago from the bite of a fiery serpent,"

Hoglah's expression changed and she looked very young and vulnerable. "Didn't the men come through here telling about the brazen serpent Moses set up?" she asked them.

"Yes, they came, but Father wouldn't let us take him to look to it and be healed," said Noah.

Tirzah spoke. "That's when he apologized and told us we were good and obedient daughters. He was so sweet and loving to us; Milcah and I had never seen him like that.

"Both he and Aunt Hasenuah were dying when Uncle Joseph brought her here on a litter to tell Father what she had done. After he heard her confess, he changed back into the father we knew when we were children," Mahlah added.

Hoglah said, almost as if to herself, "He is the one who should have been the Revenger of Blood."

The girls looked questioningly at her, not understanding what she was talking about, but Joseph knew and understood the term she used.

"Hoglah, Zelophehad was told the Amalekites did the murders—he didn't know about Hasenuah."

"What is the Revenger of Blood?" Milcah asked the question for all of them.

"It is the ancient custom that the next of kin has the right to execute the killer of his loved one," Joseph explained. "Where did you hear of it, Hoglah?"

"I heard some men talking in my father's tent about a week ago. They were discussing what God instructed Moses to do when he divides our new land unto the tribes once we enter. They said God will have cities throughout the land called Cities of Refuge. These will be given to the Levites. A person who kills someone can run to one of these cities and be safe from the Revenger until he stands trial as long he stays within the city.

"When I had an opportunity, I asked my father about the Revenger of Blood and after he explained I vowed to myself I would avenge the blood of my little brother—and that's why I came. When it happened I was just a child, frightened almost out of my mind. I had heard there always had to be two witnesses. I knew no one would take my word against the murderer—so I ran.

"But now I am a woman and I am strong and not afraid so I came to do the duty of the Revenger of Blood. Now I find Jehovah God has done the work for me. I am glad. I am relieved and glad to be with my sisters again."

Chapter 10

Israel abode still in Shittim and things were with the sisters as if Hoglah had never been away. When Asriel heard that Hoglah had returned home, he came for one of his now regular conferences with them. Asriel knew all about what they owned and helped them make business decisions and carry them out.

Hoglah loved and trusted him just as the other four did. She noted how manly he had become since she had last seen him. She could see he was still devoted to Noah. She thought Noah was silly for not feeling the same way toward him. She had been told all about Malcham and all about Hezron, but she couldn't imagine a man who fit the ideal of a husband better than this kind and helpful cousin.

When Asriel heard about her other family he agreed someone should go immediately to tell them she was safe and well. He offered to go.

"Oh Asriel, will you?" Hoglah was so grateful. "But I think I must go with you and explain to them and make sure they know how much I love and appreciate them."

"I think that is only right, Hoglah." He was glad to see she was not ungrateful. But I think if you go with me, someone else should also go." He looked at her sisters for confirmation.

"I'll go," said Noah. "I'd like to meet her other family."

"Why don't we just all go and let them meet us, too?" laughed Milcah.

Noah looked at Mahlah. "What do you think?"

"I think I'll go," said Mahlah.

"And so will I," said the youngest since no one was asking her. Thus, the matter was settled.

When Joseph heard of the plan, he told Asriel what he and Noah and Milcah had encountered in the Reubenite camp. "I think that I should send at least one of my sons or go with you myself."

Asriel knew his uncle was right; conditions were getting worse each day.

"Why not let Helek come along? I know he greatly admires Mahlah and would enjoy the trip rather than resent being sent."

Joseph laughed. He knew Helek would jump at the chance to be with Zelophehad's daughters. "I can spare him. I'll ask him to come and talk to you."

This journey was a joyful one—more like a holiday and celebration than a duty. The only thing marring the trip was the ever-present Midianites and the Israelites that had openly gone over to Baal-peor and seemed to be flaunting their new ways in the face of the ones who were maintaining the way Moses had laid out for them and their allegiance to their God, Jehovah.

The girls were grateful to have two strong men of the tribe of Manasseh as escorts. Hoglah shuddered to think she had actually ventured out into such a perilous atmosphere to carry out the role of the Revenger of Blood, and thanked God for keeping her safe.

Aside from these things, the whole group enjoyed the trip immensely. Upon arrival, they were greeted so enthusiastically it crowned the whole effort. Anthah and Reuben had indeed been frantic at the disappearance of Hoglah. Every day they and their sons went out to inquire and search for Hoglah! Her brothers were as fearful as their parents for her well-being.

After hugs and tears and explanations and laughter, Hoglah introduced her sisters and her cousins. Anthah immediately took the other four motherless ones to her bosom and they responded by loving her in return.

"God is blessing us so!" Milcah declared and all that heard, agreed. Reuben also took them under his wing. He was a little bedazzled by them. He knew more about boys than girls. But he managed to show them love and they responded in kind.

Hoglah was more than happy to share her family with them. The brothers accepted these four new sisters as easily as they had taken in Hoglah several years before. Soon they were teasing and bantering with them just as they did with Hoglah. This was something very new to the daughters of Zelophehad, and they enjoyed it immensely.

They found it hard to believe they had such peace and happiness at last. Their cups were running over.

The visit stretched into a week. Finally Asriel and Helek came to them with notice they must start back home. "We've already stayed longer than we planned—than we told Uncle Joseph. He'll be sending out searchers to find us," Asriel told them. "Hoglah, do you want to stay or go back with us?"

Hoglah was torn between staying with these dear people who had taken her in and been so kind, and going back to the life of a daughter of the tribe of Manasseh. She knew she would be guaranteed a happy life with Anthah and Reuben and the brothers, but there was something drawing her back to take her place with her tribe and her sisters.

"Now Mother, don't cry," she told Anthah. "I'll be coming regularly to visit you and Father. She took Reuben's big hand and squeezed it. "It will be the same as if I had married one of those men you've been presenting to me. I just feel somehow, there is a reason for me to go with my sisters now."

"Oh, Hoglah, I will miss you every minute," cried Anthah, "I have always believed you were a gift from God. But I, too, believe there is some reason you must go back to Manasseh. I feel it must be so. But, dear girl, don't forget us." She began to weep. Hoglah put her arms around her mother and wept with her—assuring her she would come back.

There followed a hurried preparation for the journey home and then a confusion of embraces among the brothers and sisters and cousins and parents and, when this was finally over, a sad departure—so different from the happy arrival.

As they took their journey home, they encountered several different crowds of people following men being hauled away to appear before the judges. The people following the arresting officers were loud and defiant, shouting threats and cursing. The young travelers had never seen anything like this in the camps of Israel. The girls were frightened. Helek and Asriel were very anxious to get their charges safely home.

When darkness fell they decided not to try to sleep but to continue walking, taking several wary rest stops during the dark hours. As they moved into the outer edges of the Manassite camp, they began to hear sounds of weeping and moaning and grieving coming from the tents as they passed by.

Asriel and Helek decided to go by the business district of the camp to see if they could find out what was happening. They all suspected it had to do with the Midianites and Baal-peor.

Helek told Asriel, "Remember my father's warning about that place in the Reubenite camp. We must not take the girls in. If you'd like, I'll stay with them on the outer edge and you can go in and inquire, or you can stay and I'll go in."

As Helek spoke, they rounded a turn that took them by several tents and came face-to-face with seven poles set in the ground. Upon each pole hung the body of a man. They all stopped in their tracks. The sisters shrank back and closed ranks.

"Helek! Look! That's Aramiah—and Uroch—and," Asriel's voice trailed off. He knew them all. They were prominent men of their tribe.

"The judgment has begun," Helek answered. "That's what was about to happen to the men we saw being taken in by the officers! We had better hurry. And I don't think we should take our cousins much nearer to the market."

Going a little further, they came upon a crowd surrounding several young Israelite girls who were rolling around on the ground. It was obvious they were in terrible pain. Weeping older women were kneeling beside them attempting to minister to them. Frightened young children were screaming and crying.

Milcah and her sisters noticed the suffering girls' clothing was different from the usual garb of the Israelite women. They had attempted to copy the colorful dress of the happy-go-lucky Midianites. Now both they and their gay attire were being covered with the dust of the Manassite campground.

Then came other solemn people passing by them carrying their loved ones on litters to the tents. They could plainly see that the stricken ones were of all ages from teenagers to elders. Some were screaming and writhing in pain; some were deathly pale and silent. The din of grieving was coming from all around them now and growing louder.

Asriel halted his little company. "Helek, you stay here and I'll run ahead. I'll get back as quickly as I can. If I'm not back within a very short time, take the girls on to their home." Helek nodded assent and Asriel ran away.

Mahlah instructed her sisters to sit on some rocks at the side of the path that ran through the camp. "Get as far back and out of the way as you can," she said. Her eyes were huge, and wide open in fear and alarm. They sat and she settled next to them. Helek positioned himself in front of them and between them and the path.

He smiled what he hoped was a reassuring smile at them. "Don't worry, we'll be all right. But I think it would be a good idea for you to cover your faces." They obeyed by pulling their veils up and over their shining hair.

"I'm almost sure I know what is happening now, and if it is what I think, we're in no danger. Not one of us has turned from Jehovah to their god, Baal-peor!"

The girls were still and quiet. They couldn't get rid of all the awful things they had seen. The image of seven of their own familiar neighbors hanging on seven poles in the bright sunlight of the plains of Moab was stamped forever in their hearts.

Just as Helek was about to tell his cousins they must go on, Asriel came running back to them from between some nearby tents. "It's as we guessed. Moses was ordered by Jehovah to kill all the heads of our people who have joined themselves to Baal-peor and to hang them before the sun for all to look at and think on what disobeying Jehovah

will bring about."

Asriel bent over from the waist with hands on his thighs, trying to catch his breath. "And," he finished, "the plague has stricken people all around us—the people who turned their back to our God and began to worship the gods of Moab and Midian."

Helek said, "We knew judgment would surely come. I am just surprised that Jehovah was so longsuffering in this matter." He turned to his cousins. "Let us go home! We have nothing to fear if we keep His commandments."

A very worried Joseph was waiting at Zelophehad's tent for them. "I am so thankful that you are all home safely. I knew you had nothing to fear from God in the matter of Baal-peor. But I feared that some of the ones who had joined themselves to that way might have harmed you before the arrests and the plague began!" He embraced his beloved oldest son Helek, then Asriel and then his brother's daughters, one-by-one.

I thank Jehovah I woke up and stopped my daughters from going to those feasts before they were completely won over to that disgusting way! They came so close because I did not pay attention as I should. They could be dying that awful death at this moment. I think they have learned. I hope they've learned.

Chapter 11

The plague continued a few more days and then suddenly there were no new cases. Later they learned what had happened.

The Midianites had become so bold when they had won over so many of the leaders in the tribes of Israel that they had dared to set up a tent (such as the one Reuben and Noah and Milcah had seen in Reuben). It was so close to the tabernacle that it could easily be seen by the people who visited the place where Jehovah God said he would meet with His people. This tabernacle was surrounded by a white linen fence. And the glory cloud of God stood over it day and night.

One day after the plague had taken many people there was a huge crowd of weeping Israelites gathered at the door in the white linen fence. These mourners heard a cheer rise up from the men around the Midianite tent and saw Zimri, the son of Sallu, a prince of a chief house among the Simeonites arriving at the Midianite tent and showing off a beautiful and gorgeously arrayed woman to those standing by.

Phineas, who was the son of Eleazar, the high priest of Israel, saw the Israelite man and the Midianite woman entering the tent. He leapt up from among the congregation and took a javelin in his hand. He ran through the crowd around the tabernacle and on through the crowd at the tent of Baal-peor worship. Those arrogant men saw him follow Zimri and the woman into the tent. There, Phineas thrust the javelin through both of them—the man of Israel and the strange woman through her belly.

The plague was immediately stayed. Jehovah told Moses that Phineas' act had turned away His wrath in jealousy from the children of Israel because the young priest was zealous for Jehovah's sake among them.

The woman who died with the Simeonite, Zimri, turned out to be Cozbi, the daughter of Zur, who was of one of the chief houses of Midian and the head over many Midianites.

Following this, Jehovah ordered Moses to vex the Midianites and smite them. He ordered Moses to take the sum of all the congregation of Israel from twenty years and upward throughout their fathers' houses, all that were able to go to war.

Of the families of Manasseh, those that were numbered were fifty-two thousand and seven hundred. Compared to the numbers of some of the other tribes, that was small. But when time came for fighting, they had an equal part in the war with the Midianites.

Jehovah spoke to Moses and told him to avenge the children of Israel of the Midianites and after that was done he was to prepare to die.

Moses spoke to the Israelites saying they should arm one thousand men of each tribe for war. That made an army of twelve thousand. None of the younger men the daughters of Zelophehad knew were called this time, but Joseph volunteered. Indeed he asked the leaders to send him and they agreed.

This small army warred against the Midianites as Jehovah had commanded and they killed all the males. Among them were five kings, Evi, Rekem, Zur, Hur, and Reba. Also the prophet Balaam, the son of Beor was slain by the sword of Israel.

They burnt all the cities and goodly castles and took all the spoil—cattle, flocks, gold, silver, brass, iron, tin, and lead. They took women and children captives and brought them to Moses and Eleazar the priest and the congregation of the children of Israel, to the camp at the plains of Moab, which are by the Jordan near Jericho.

Moses and Eleazar and all the princes of the congregation went out to meet them. When Moses saw the captives he became very angry with the captains over thousands and the captains over hundreds in the army. He asked them if they did not understand that the women of Midian had been used through the counsel of Balaam to cause Israel to sin against Jehovah and had brought about the plague as God's judgment.

He ordered them to kill all the male children and all the women that had had sexual relations with Midianite men. They were to spare only the girl children who had not had sexual relations.

He gave them orders on how to purify both themselves and their captives. Anyone who had killed and anyone who had touched a dead body were to be cleansed on the third and again on the seventh day. They were to purify their clothing also.

Moses and Eleazar then instructed the warriors how all the spoil they had taken was to be purified and exactly how it was to be divided with those who had not gone out to fight—even to the tabernacle itself.

After the days of purification were over and the spoil divided as directed, the officers of the army—captains over hundreds and captains over thousands—came to Moses with a special offering.

They said they had taken count of the men that had been under their command and had found not one was missing. The offering was made up of gold and jewelry they had personally taken during the fighting. It came to 16,750 shekels and Moses brought it to the tabernacle to be a memorial for the children of Israel before the LORD.

After the fighting was done and the camps clear of the Midianites, the people turned their attention to practical matters. They wanted to get on with their lives; they were looking to the time when God would lead them across the Jordan.

The men of the tribes of Reuben, Gad, and half of the tribe of Manasseh had maintained the tradition of keeping herds and flocks from the time of their fathers, Abraham, Isaac and Jacob. This was the occupation of Jacob's sons when they had been brought into Egypt by their brother Joseph who had risen to the position of second ruler in that land.

As they had fought their way through the land of the Amorites, the men of these tribes had noted that the land of Sihon and Og was a land especially suited to the keeping of animals. They had discussed it several times among themselves since they had passed through it, and a decision was made by the leaders to ask Moses if they could keep this land instead of taking a portion on the west side of Jordan.

They formulated a plan whereby they would send the fighting men of the tribe across the Jordan with the rest of Israel to fight until the land had all been secure. But, they were to leave the rest of their tribes on the east to occupy the cities and villages and the countryside which had made up the realms of the two Amorite kings.

Asriel came to consult with his cousins over this matter. They were the heirs of Zelophehad and thus would be entitled to a larger piece of land than Joseph, Machir, and Shemiah, his brothers.

"I think you should be represented in the next meeting where this is discussed. It means that you—unless you sell your sheep and cattle—would have to remain east of the river and take your inheritance here," Asriel informed them.

Noah, who had become bored with housekeeping and had returned to being a shepherd after peace and safety had been restored to the camps, knew all about the meetings their tribal leaders had been conducting with those of Reuben and Gad. She told her sisters, "We are going to have to speak up now if we are against this plan. They are going to talk to Moses and Eleazar very soon, because we all feel the time is coming when Israel will be going into Canaan.

"I see nothing wrong with the proposal if our fighting men will go before therest of Israel fighting and conquering as if we were to live over there when it is pronounced finished."

Asriel nodded his agreement and looked to the others for any dissent. "We don't even know if God will allow Moses to agree to the plan, but I am like Noah—I can't see anything wrong with it. There is no doubt that this land would be ideal for keeping our animals."

"Will it not cut us off from our kinsmen?" asked Milcah. There will be the river—a natural barrier—between us."

Mahlah nodded.

"It won't unless we allow it," Noah answered thoughtfully. This had not occurred to her. We'd have to work at keeping close relations with them."

"But, would we?" Hoglah was thinking out loud.

"And the biggest problem would be that we would be across the river from the tabernacle and the presence of Jehovah," Milcah told them. "It would be further temptation to grow away from our God and our people."

"I go along with what our leaders are telling us," Tirzah announced. "I say we send word to them that we think it's a good plan."

Mahlah agreed. "We wouldn't know what to do without our cattle and sheep. But we must also voice our concern that we could become alienated from the rest of Israel."

Asriel had sat listening and found their discussion had thrown new light on his attitude toward the proposal. "Joseph and I will be going to another meeting tomorrow. Which of you wants to come and speak your position? Remember, some of the men will not like your being there," he warned.

"I think Mahlah and Hoglah should go," said Noah. "Mahlah is so dignified and Hoglah will not be afraid to stand up to the leaders. I'd rather be with the sheep."

"I agree," said Milcah. "I don't think I'd like to do it, but I would if I had to." She looked to Tirzah for confirmation.

"I guess I agree," said the youngest, "but I really don't have strong feelings about it. Let Mahlah and Hoglah go."

Hoglah and Noah went with their kinsmen to the meeting next day. Surprisingly, there was no open opposition to their being there. The men listened as Hoglah and then Mahlah told them their ideas about the plan.

Many of them had not considered this might cause an alienation from the other tribes. It was something that could turn into a serious problem.

Mahlah and Hoglah returned to the others feeling a little proud of having participated in the meeting. But the ones who stayed behind soon took it all out of them by teasing and pointing out that they had only carried the ideas of the whole group, "which anyone could have done." But in their hearts they admired the way Mahlah and Hoglah had performed. Asriel had openly praised the two for the way they had conducted themselves and carried out their mission.

This venture into the world brought about a great change in the everyday life of Zelophehad's daughters. Five days after the meeting, it began at mid-morning. Two men hailed them from outside the tent. Tirzah went to the door. These men were from the tribe of Gad and wanted to meet with Mahlah and Hoglah. She invited them in.

After the greetings the men stated their reason for the visit. They had come to propose marriage, the older one to Mahlah, the younger to Hoglah.

"We talked with your uncle, because we knew your father had died," said the older of the two. "Joseph said we had to talk to you; that you and your sisters are responsible for each other."

The younger man told them they had made a very favorable impression at the meeting. "Not only do I think Hoglah is very pretty, but she struck me as being very sensible and responsible. Joseph explained your situation and said we should come and consult with you personally."

Milcah and Tirzah stood to the side, listening. They could not keep from giggling, seeing the startled looks on the faces of their sisters. The younger man turned to them and smiled, noting they were just as attractive as the older sisters. "We are serious," he said. "Have you had any other visitors from our tribe?"

Mahlah laughed, "No, you are the first."

The older man said, "My cousin here is serious. We know of several that are interested in you. You had a very favorable reputation before we saw you at the meeting."

They continued the conversation telling their names and lineage and what they had to offer. Hoglah and Mahlah finally got into the seriousness of the proposals and gave them the respect they deserved. After the discussion Hoglah told them, "This is all such a surprise to us; we need time to inquire about you and then consider."

The men smiled and assured that they would come back in about a month or so to learn the decision. They were delighted not to have been rejected outright. The older man pressed his case. "Please remember my name,

149

Mahlah, and what I've told you. I know you are going to have other offers and I want you to remember me."

Mahlah and Hoglah were laughing and their faces were flushed with excitement and pleasure.

"That goes for me, also," the one seeking Hoglah's consent told her.

The girls showed them to the door and waved pleasant goodbyes.

This was the beginning of a flood of visitors resulting from the meeting they had attended. There followed four more suitors for Mahlah and three more for Hoglah.

When Helek learned from Joseph about all these inquiries, he said, "Father, I want to marry Mahlah. I have been waiting for her to recover from learning about Hezron, but it looks as if I had better speak up now."

So Joseph accompanied Helek to Zelophehad's tent for a serious talk with the sisters about the possibility of Mahlah's marriage to him. By now, her head was swimming with all the proposals. It was hard for her to believe she was the object of all this attention.

Joseph very seriously presented the formal offer for his oldest son. But Helek stated his own case very simply, "I love you, Mahlah," he said. "I've loved you for a long time but have not spoken about it for reasons you well know. Now that others have met you and are coming with their proposals, I decided I must bring mine to you also."

"I can't think of anyone I'd rather see my son marry, Mahlah," Joseph said as he rose to leave. "Maybe he could make up a little for what has happened to you. I know he would be good to you."

Noah, Hoglah, Milcah, and Tirzah were all smiling their approval as they said their goodbyes and saw their kinsmen out the tent door.

Mahlah still sat in her place. Helek had never given her the slightest indication of how he felt. She suddenly saw him in a new light.

Chapter 12

The stream of visitors had by no means ended. Very soon after Helek's proposal there came five more men to Zelophehad's tent. These were older men with stern and serious looks. Mahlah and Hoglah recognized them as having taken part in the meeting they had attended—in fact, one of them had conducted the meeting.

They informed Mahlah that they had not come far and refused the foot washing greeting. She asked them, "Will you sit down then and tell us why you are here?" She indicated the reed crate seats and their one divan. When they were all seated with the girls standing attentively by, the man who seemed to be the leader spoke. "We have met with Moses and he has accepted our proposal to send our fighting men into The Land at the head of the other tribes, but the rest of our two and one-half tribes will stay and inhabit the land of Sihon and Og."

The girls waited, not knowing what response was expected of them.

"But," the man said, "we have come to talk to you about the land that would have been allotted to your father or his son."

"We are his heirs," Noah stated firmly.

"Wait," one of the other men answered. "We know you are entitled to his money, goods, animals, and whatever else he owned. But this land Moses will be dividing to us is a different matter."

"Why should it be different?" Hoglah demanded.

"Because it hasn't been divided yet and your father has died," another man explained patiently, as if they were children.

Noah glared at him. "Do you expect to receive the land that would have gone to your father if he were still alive?" she asked.

"Yes," he said, "but that is different."

"How so?" asked Milcah.

"Well," he said, "because I am his heir, along with my brothers."

"Of just his money, goods, animals, and whatever else he owned?" asked Milcah again.

"No, the land that will come to the tribe that would have been divided to him will be given to me and my brothers." He spoke very slowly so they could be sure to understand.

Mahlah stepped around in front of him. "That is the very same situation we are in," she said very slowly, mimicking his tone and manner.

He stood up angrily. "But it is not the same!" His voice was louder and he forgot to speak slowly.

Noah stepped up to stand beside Mahlah and grinned at him. "How does it differ?" She wanted him to *say* it.

"Because it should go to the male heirs!" he almost shouted.

All five of the daughters of Zelophehad laughed. It upset the visitors mightily.

The other men stood up. Their leader said, "We came here to try to help you! But we cannot if you will not cooperate."

"By doing what?" asked Hoglah. "By giving up the right to our father's inheritance in Manasseh? We don't need that kind of help!"

The leader started toward the door. "We'll see about that," he told them as the five stalked out of the tent.

The girls sat down and stared at each other. "What next?" asked Hoglah. "Life around Zelophehad's tent is never boring."

Tirzah stood up. "I don't believe Jehovah God will allow them to steal our part of the land. We should pray and then go ask Moses to speak to God on our account."

Thus another journey came about—and this one all-important. It was difficult to believe they were actually going to speak with the great man Moses.

The camps were quiet and peaceful now and they could have safely gone by themselves, but Joseph asked if he could accompany them. Of course, they were glad to have him come along.

The walk through one side of the Israelite encampment took them two and one- half days. They did not try to hurry and being free of stress and fear, they enjoyed their trip.

The girls laughed and talked together as they proceeded. The people they met seemed relaxed and happy. Many of them greeted the five attractive young women and stopped to look after them when they had passed. There was something compelling about the group.

Joseph knew people assumed he was the father of these five and that suited him well. He was very proud of them.

As they neared the center of the whole Israelite encampment on the third day, the five daughters of Zelophehad were awe-stricken. There, brilliant in the sunlight of the plains of Moab, was the white linen fence that surrounded the tabernacle. They had never before seen it.

The shining column of cloud—the Shekinah Glory of God—stood directly over the small animal skin covered tent which appeared weather-worn and not really appealing to the human eye from the outside. Smoke ascended from the brazen altar of burnt offerings which was just inside the ornate and colorful blue and purple and scarlet embroidered hangings which made up the door of the fence.

There was the smell of burning fat and animal flesh in the air, and they could hear the lowing of the cattle and the bleating of the sheep people were bringing to be sacrificed by the priests.

The fence was tall enough to prevent their seeing what went on in the enclosure.

The young women slackened their pace and then came to a halt just to take in the significance of this small tent surrounded by the white linen fence.

The column of cloud was hugely impressive, but they had seen it many times when it lifted and went before them in the wilderness.

But to actually be at the place where their Jehovah God had promised to dwell between the cherubim on the mercy seat was overwhelming. Joseph stood by quietly while his nieces collected themselves. For once, there was no talking among them. They just stood, each absorbing the sights, sounds, and smells emanating from this holy place.

There was a crowd of people gathered in the space in front of the tabernacle obscuring the opening in the fence.

Finally Hoglah said, "I wonder how we will find Moses." This was the question they were all pondering.

"He must be in this crowd of people," Joseph told them. Many come to him to settle matters.

As they continued, they saw more and more people walking toward the place where the crowd had assembled. Joseph asked a man who passed them walking away from the crowd, "Excuse me, sir, could you tell me where we can find Moses?"

The man didn't stop walking, but pointed back toward the crowd. "He's in the middle of all those people."

"Could you tell me if we . . . ?" Joseph began his next question, but the man had hurried on his way. Joseph and the girls kept moving. Each was wondering what procedure one must follow to gain an audience.

But as they drew nearer they saw how it was working. There were men on the outskirts of the area who met and questioned new arrivals and assigned them places in what at first had seemed just a milling group of people. They even marked a place where people exited and walked away.

Then one of the "screeners" approached them. "Are you here to talk with Moses?" he asked. Joseph opened his mouth to answer, but Hoglah spoke before him, "We are five women, sisters, from the tribe of Manasseh. We have come to petition for inheritance of the land that would have been allotted to our father, Zelophehad, if he had lived to receive it."

The eyes of the big man widened and Milcah thought she could see a trace of a smile on his face when he heard Hoglah's words.

"Have you taken your petition before the judges and rulers of the tribe of Manasseh?" He was required to ask the people this question. If the case had been already judged and the petitioners just didn't like the decision, they were usually turned away so Moses would not be completely inundated.

"The judges and rulers of our tribe are the ones trying to take the right away from us," Hoglah again spoke for the group.

"Oh," their guide said, scratching his head, "that makes it complicated. I don't like to turn people away,but your judge and your rulers say you cannot inherit, I think that settles it." He spoke in a manner that gave away his lack of conviction.

Mahlah caught it. She smiled at the man; for some reason she had decided he must be a Levite—she had no idea why. "Have you had similar cases?" she asked him politely.

"To tell you the truth," he said, returning her smile, "I've never heard of such a thing. But then, dividing up this land our God has promised us is going to be a whole new issue."

Tirzah stepped around to the front of the group. She, too, smiled at the big man. Tirzah liked everybody (until they gave her reason not to) and people could sense it. "Sir, I told my sisters that Jehovah God would not allow men to take away our inheritance; that we should come and ask Moses to ask God for us."

The Levite nodded. "I'll take you to Moses. Since we have no instructions in a case like this—maybe the LORD has given him something to go by. Come, follow me."

He led them along to a place in the crowd that moved forward at long intervals. He inserted them just ahead of some people another Levite was bringing to place in the slowly advancing slot.

"Just keep moving forward and you will get there eventually." He spoke kindly and he received five brilliantly smiling "thank you's" from the girls and a pat on the shoulder from the beaming man who accompanied them.

Joseph was relieved and pleased they had found their way and negotiated so easily for this chance. He had secretly carried a little knot of fear in his belly, not knowing how to go about securing an audience with the leader of Israel.

The afternoon wore on and on. Sometimes they would advance several steps rapidly; sometimes it took long minutes before they could move at all. They soon realized that not all the people in the crowd were petitioners. Some had only come to see Moses in action and to be entertained by the hearing of the pleas and the solution their great leader pronounced.

The strong Levites kept them all moving toward Moses and when a petitioner was answered and dismissed, the Levites moved the front row of onlookers out with him. No one was allowed to stay long in the front row. These were the people they had observed exiting regularly.

At last they moved into a place where they could see Moses. He was sitting on a plain wooden bench and another man was seated at his right hand. It was Eleazar, Aaron's oldest son, who had inherited the office of high priest when his father died.

The scene was nothing like they had imagined it would be. There was a clay water pot with some cups on the ground next to Moses. There was an adjustable movable awning shading the bench from the sun, and there were three of the big Levites standing on each side. Behind Moses stood a man holding a javelin. He gave the impression of being very strong. His black hair was streaked with gray. He watched Moses very intently.

Also, seated behind Moses, between him and the linen fence of the tabernacle—and under more portable awnings—sat about a dozen important-looking men who also watched and listened intently to the proceedings.

Somehow they had expected Moses to be feeble, but he was not. His beard and hair were snow white, but his body seemed to be as full of strength as those of the younger men around him. He rose to walk back and forth—as relief from sitting so long—and they could see he was tall and straight, and he was also as big as his Levite brothers.

He stopped to listen to the next petitioner and his whole attention centered on what that person was telling him.

Suddenly, the decision had been made and the men ahead of them led away and they stood before Moses, who had once again taken his seat. They stepped up and stood silent. The girls had forgotten to decide who would speak. Moses raised his eyes and looked questioningly at them. Then a hint of a smile crossed his face. They were a pleasing picture, a welcome change from the angry and contentious people he had been dealing with all day.

The smile broke forth on his face and he asked in a gracious manner, "Which of you is going to tell me your problem?" They looked at each other and ended up with all eyes on Mahlah, nodding their consensus that she should speak. The four younger moved almost imperceptibly back.

Mahlah was not surprised; she believed she should speak since she was the oldest. She took a deep breath. Moses' kindly eyes were encouraging her and she began. "We are five daughters of Zelophehad, the son of Hepher, of the tribe of Manasseh." She looked to the side to see her Uncle Joseph who was smiling proudly and nodding approval she should go on.

"Our father died in the wilderness, and he was not in the company of them that gathered themselves together against the LORD in the company of Korah; but he died in his sins and had no sons. Why should the name of our father be done away from among his family, because he hath no son? Give unto us *therefore* a possession among the brethren of our father." (Numbers 27:3-4 KJV)

Mahlah's statement caused a wave of little gasps and ripples of whispering among the crowd and among those men who sat behind Moses. Noah, Hoglah, Milcah, and Tirzah stepped back up and stood two on each side of Mahlah, strong and unmoving. Joseph also moved closer to them.

The great leader Moses laughed, pleased at the courage of these five young Israelite women. "Why indeed?" He spoke strongly, making sure that all present heard him.

And Tirzah said, "I told my sisters I didn't believe that Jehovah God would allow men to take away our possession in the land that will be given to our tribe. I said we should come to ask you to ask the LORD what you should do for us!"

"That is exactly what I must do, my dear," Moses agreed, "because I don't know the answer." He looked to Eleazar and then to the men behind him, "We will adjourn for an hour and I will ask God what must be done." Then he said to all, "Be back in an hour. This is a very serious question that will affect all of Israel. I want you leaders to hear God's answer from my lips, so it cannot be doubted."

With that, he picked up his staff from the bench and strode toward the tabernacle.

The extra hour of waiting did not seem so difficult to the daughters of Zelophehad because they had seen and experienced so many things that day. They had actually appeared before and spoken with the great man Moses. They had seen the high priest, Eleazar; they had seen the tabernacle!

The people around them seemed to enjoy watching them as they talked excitedly. Joseph finally just sat on the ground in his place. Noah decided that was the sensible thing to do after being on her feet for hours. She sat beside him. Then Tirzah and Milcah, and finally Hoglah sat. It felt good. All these four had been shepherds and accustomed to sitting on the ground at times.

Mahlah moved nervously around them. "Get up girls! This is so unladylike," she fretted. "What will people think?"

"They'll probably think we have good common sense, Mahlah," Milcah told her.

"See?" asked Noah, pointing to several people around them who had followed their lead. Mahlah gave in and sat between Noah and Hoglah—she was hoping no one she knew would see her. Her sisters grinned at each other, *Whom did they know around here?*

Soon Moses came back. The strong-looking man carrying the javelin was close by his side. Everyone stood. The little murmur swept through the assembly again as Moses took his seat. Then Eleazar and the men behind Moses sat down. Moses turned and spoke over his shoulder to the man with the javelin who, in turn, spoke to the dozen behind him. Those men stopped their murmuring and gave close attention.

Moses spoke in an unusually loud voice. "This is the answer God has given me!" His eyes came to rest upon Tirzah, who was smiling at him.

"The daughters of Zelophehad speak right: thou shalt surely give them a possession of an inheritance among their father's brethren; and thou shalt cause the inheritance of their father to pass unto them.

"And thou shalt speak unto the children of Israel, saying, If a man die and have no son, then ye shall cause his inheritance to pass unto his daughter.

"And if he have no daughter, then ye shall give his inheritance unto his brethren.

"And if he have no brethren, then ye shall give his inheritance to his father's brethren.

"And if his father have no brethren, then ye shall give his inheritance unto his kinsman that is next to him of his family, and he shall possess it: and it shall be unto the children of Israel a statute of judgment, as the LORD commanded Moses." (Numbers 27:7-11 KJV)

The girls sent up a little cheer of victory and hugged each other and their Uncle Joseph. The men behind Moses frowned and looked serious. Joshua (for he was the strong man standing behind Moses) smiled and made a salute to the five with his javelin.

Moses looked upon them once more with a very gracious smile. Then he signaled the Levites to usher them out.

"Next petitioner," they heard someone call as they were led out of the way.

Chapter 13

Soon after the daughters' visit to the tabernacle area, God gave Moses instructions concerning his death. He was told to go up into the mount Abarim to view the land which God had given to Israel. After he had seen it, he was told he would be gathered unto his people as his brother Aaron had been before him. God told him the reason he was not allowed to enter the land: "For ye rebelled against my commandment in the desert of Zin, in the strife of the congregation, to sanctify me at the water before their eyes: that *is* the water of Meribah in Kadesh in the wilderness of Zin." (Numbers 27:14 KJV)

As always, Moses' concern was for the people he had led so long. He told God that, without him the Israelites would be like sheep without a shepherd. But God was far ahead of him. He told Moses to take Joshua, the son of Nun, in whom was His Spirit and after he had laid his hand on him, to take him and set him before Eleazar the priest and before all the congregation and give him a charge in their sight.

Moses was to put some of his honor upon Joshua so all would know they were to follow and obey Joshua after the death of Moses. Joshua was to consult with Eleazar the High Priest, who would consult God with Urim and advise Joshua as God instructed.

It was obvious to all that they would soon be crossing the river. There was an urgency about Moses as he tried to get everything done before it was time for him to die.

He called an assembly of all the leaders of the tribes and reviewed Jehovah's promises of what behavior would bring about blessings and what behavior would bring about cursings in the new land. There was not one man who left the meeting unsure of what God required of him.

But the leaders of the tribe of Manasseh had something on their minds with which Moses would have to deal. They secured an audience with Moses and the leaders of the other tribes as quickly as possible.

They told Moses that they knew that God had instructed him to give the daughters of Zelophehad an inheritance among the sons of Manasseh and they accepted that without question. But they did have questions about what would happen to that land should the women marry someone of another tribe. It could be taken from the tribe of Manasseh and placed in the inheritance of her husband's tribe when their children inherited.

This, they argued, would cause great confusion and complicate the simple division of the land according to tribe. Moses and all the other leaders had to agree this was true.

Once more Moses consulted the LORD while the leaders waited.

"And Moses commanded the children of Israel according to the word of the LORD, saying, The tribe of the sons of Joseph hath said well.

"This is the thing which the LORD doth command concerning the daughters of Zelophehad, saying, Let them marry to whom they think best; only to the family of the tribe of their father shall they marry.

"So shall not the inheritance of the children of Israel remove from tribe to tribe: for every one of the children of Israel shall keep himself to the inheritance of the tribe of his fathers.

"And every daughter, that possesseth an inheritance in any tribe of the children of Israel, shall be wife unto one of the family of the tribe of her father, that the children of Israel may enjoy every man the inheritance of his fathers.

"Neither shall the inheritance remove from tribe to tribe; but every one of the tribes of the children of Israel shall keep himself to his own inheritance. (Numbers 36:5-9 KJV)

This was a satisfactory answer to all—especially to the tribe of Manasseh—which was facing the problem immediately. After this matter had been settled, Moses gave instruction to all who needed his instruction.

Moses had completed the song he had made about Israel and their land and he spoke it to the leaders and their people. Then he blessed all the tribes. He was ready!

"And Moses went up from the plains of Moab unto the mountain of Nebo, to the top of Pisgah, that is over against Jericho. And the LORD shewed him all the land of Gilead, unto Dan.

"And all Naphtali, and the land of Ephraim, and Manasseh, and all the land of Judah, unto the utmost sea,

"And the south, and the plain of the valley of Jericho, the city of palm trees, unto Zoar.

"And the LORD said unto him, This is the land which I sware unto Abraham, unto Isaac, and unto Jacob, saying, I will give it unto thy seed: I have caused thee to see *it* with thine eyes, but thou shalt not go over thither.

"So Moses the servant of the LORD died there in the land of Moab, according to the word of the LORD.

"And he buried him in a valley in the land of Moab, over against Beth-peor: but no man knoweth of his sepulchre unto this day." (Deuteronomy 34:1-6 KJV)

The Israelites mourned for Moses for thirty days there in the camp in the plains of Moab. When the days of mourning were done, they had a new leader, Joshua, who was full of the spirit of wisdom, for Moses had laid his hands upon him.

The Israelites were willing to follow him and did as the LORD had commanded Moses. Zelophehad's daughters mourned the death of Moses with the rest of Israel. They mourned him as a great leader and they mourned him also because he had been a friend and a helper to them by taking their petition to God.

When the leaders of the tribe of Manasseh had returned after the gathering and their hearing with Moses, they put forth the answer that God had given for keeping the inheritance in the tribe. This circumstance of having no sons was rare, but now there were firm guidelines from Jehovah God, Himself, by which to meet and treat the situation.

The same delegation that had visited the sisters before came calling upon them once more. This time they found Asriel present, helping the girls with some decisions about the livestock.

Hoglah answered their call from outside. They ushered them into the tent but did not ask them to be seated or offer them hospitality. The others rose from their seats around Asriel and came to the front of the tent where they stood waiting for the men to state their business.

The leader hesitated a moment and seeing no sign of welcome, began to speak to the unsmiling women. "We have been to meet with Moses and the leaders of the other tribes."

"Yes?" said Mahlah.

The speaker was reminded by her tone, how they had been treated by these girls before. His temper began to rise and his face reddened, but he tried hard to keep control. "The decision to allow you to inherit the land has been amended." His voice took on his "official" tone. He could hardly wait to witness the let down of these arrogant young women when they found they had been limited to their own tribe.

"Yes?" This time it was Noah speaking, with the same look and attitude Mahlah had shown.

Asriel stood up and came to stand behind Noah. The other men were frowning and hoping their leader would hurry and tell these defiant ones the decision from Moses.

He spat it out, "When a woman inherits she is free to marry whom she will but the man has to be from her father's tribe!"

"Oh, I think that is just wonderful!" Tirzah exclaimed.

The men's countenances collapsed.

"That way the land will remain forever in the tribe to which it has been given! God is so wise and so good!" Milcah told them with enthusiasm.

"No man could have thought of a better solution. We do thank you for coming to inform us," said Mahlah and started to usher the disappointed guests toward the door. Hoglah followed and told them, "It was so good of you to come and let us know so quickly. Thank you again," she said as the last man filed out the door.

The daughters of Zelophehad laughed together once more.

Asriel was watching them with a questioning look on his face. "Why are you laughing?" he wanted to know.

"Oh, you would have had to witness our first encounter with them to understand," Noah told him.

Then she turned to Mahlah and said seriously, "Can you think of anyone that you would rather marry right now than a man from the tribe of Manasseh?"

Mahlah was startled at both the question and the serious way Noah had asked it. Then she thought of Helek, who had finally revealed how he had loved her for years. "No! I must admit I can't," she said emphatically, "can you?"

"No," said Noah, turning and looking into Asriel's eyes.

He was still puzzled, but it was beginning to come across that Noah was talking about him.

"I know one Manassite who has faithfully served me as a friend and a helper for years. He is handsome, and a valiant warrior, and he is a good business man, and he is kind and good, and my family loves and trusts him, and . . ."

Asriel started to laugh. He placed his hands on Noah's shoulders and peered into her face. "You are not teasing me are you, Noah? Would you really marry me?" He was so surprised and happy he was almost crying. "I have loved you so long!"

"And so well!" she answered him. "Yes, Asriel, I want to marry you right away. I want us to have a son to carry on my father's name in Israel. I want us to have many sons and daughters."

Hoglah, Milcah, and Tirzah were jumping up and down and clapping their hands for joy. Asriel grinned at them. "I assume by your response that I have your permission to marry your sister?" he asked in a formal voice.

The three charged him and all hugged him at once.

"Wait a minute!' cried Noah. "He's going to marry me!"

"Seriously, Noah," he asked, "do you mean right away? I am almost sure the other tribes will be crossing the river into Canaan very soon. I will have to go, as we have promised, with our fighting men before all Israel until the whole land Jehovah has promised us is secured." He still could not believe this was really happening.

Noah hugged him, too. "Yes, my dear, sweet Asriel. I mean now—right now—as soon as we can! We mustn't waste any more time.

"Those hateful men were hoping their news would upset us, but they actually did me a great favor and woke me up. How about you, Mahlah? Isn't there a young man of the tribe of your father that you need to talk to before Israel crosses Jordan and he has to go to the fight?"

Asriel was excited now. "I must go tell my father! Is he ever going to be surprised? He has given me up; he thought I was never going to marry. I must go and make arrangements for the marriage—and a place for us to live—and . . ." He was pulling Noah along with him to the door.

Mahlah caught his sleeve as he passed her. "Will you tell Helek that I want to see him right away?"

"I'll tell him if I can remember," he said. "I am so excited I can't promise I'll remember anything!"

He stopped and put his arms around Noah and kissed her. Then he gave a shout and went running away.

Chapter 14

Noah became the wife of Asriel and Mahlah became the wife of Helek on the same day—married to men of the house of their father. Asriel temporarily moved in with Noah and the younger sisters and the triumphant Helek carried the glowingly happy Mahlah off to the place he had prepared for her in his father's house.

(Joseph could not help but think of how his wife, Hasenuah, had so tragically schemed and even killed, to obtain the greater inheritance of his brother Zelophehad and now that very thing had been brought about through the love of his son for Zelophehad's oldest daughter.)

Israel now set itself to await the word from its leader Joshua that the time had come to enter The Land. When it finally came to Manasseh in the form of a reminder from Joshua that they had promised their fighting men would go on before their brothers, it was still a shock.

Joseph, Asriel, Helek—all the able-bodied men above twenty years had to go. That meant the women and younger men would have to take on the work of the ones going to war.

Israelites who had been accountable in the refusal to enter The Land about forty years ago at Kadesh-barnea had, except for Joshua and Caleb, all died as God had said in the wilderness. So there were few older men who would be left behind to assist in the everyday work the warriors were leaving.

The length of the conquest was left up to the conquerors. God had promised them victory, but the children of Israel had to go in and claim it. Little did Reuben, Gad, and the half of the tribe of Manasseh guess when they marched away from their loved ones and this newly acquired land that they would not return to dwell there permanently for seven years.

The day of the departure of the Manasseh warriors came much too soon for all concerned. Asriel tried to find younger men to help his new wife and her sisters with their livestock, but everyone was now having the same problem—lack of manpower.

Fortunately, Zelophehad's daughters had worked all their lives—and were capable. But now the hours would be longer and the work harder. They wondered how the women who had always been coddled and pampered were going to cope.

"They'll just have to learn the hard way, I guess," Noah told them.

That was not the part that was worrying her. Now that she had decided to put away the sad loss of Malcham and get on with life, she found that she loved Asriel very dearly. She was so happy she could hardly stand the thought of his leaving now.

How she prayed she would be carrying his child when he left. She wouldn't let herself consider the possibility that he might be killed in battle. She savored every moment they had together and there was not a happier man in all Israel than Asriel of Manasseh.

Helek may have been the second happiest. He was so proud to have won the hand of one of the richest and surely, the most beautiful and eligible women in their tribe. He had thought through the years that there was no way the son of the woman who hated her mother and father and killed their baby son could hope to marry Mahlah. It was a miracle to him and he treated her like a princess.

Mahlah had found her niche. She had always aspired only to be a wife and mother in Israel. She also hoped and prayed that Jehovah would allow her to conceive a child before Helek had to leave to enter The Land.

Joseph had three sons going to war. He had a daughter whose husband was still young enough to stay behind and help the women. He had another daughter and three sons who would have to take over the work of the men. He was so glad to have Mahlah in his household to oversee things and watch after his younger children. War made things so complicated.

Hoglah, Milcah, and Tirzah took this all in stride. They had been born into troubles and lived in them most of their young lives. They were more content than they had ever been.

Seeing their older sisters so happy in marriage encouraged them to think they, too, would be able to find the right ones for them from the house of Zelophehad's fathers. Not one of them was anxious to be married, but from the meeting of Manasseh and their petition and answer from God and Moses, they knew the offers would be coming soon.

There were still plenty of young cousins going to be left at home from which to choose. There was no urgency to be found in the three of them. *After all*, they thought, *look how well Mahlah and Noah have done for themselves and they are past the age of twenty!*

The dreaded day finally came. The fighting men of the half tribe of Manasseh were to gather on the outside edge of their camp, organize, march through the commercial area, and out to hook up with the men of Reuben and Gad. Then all would march on to the tabernacle to follow the priests bearing the ark across the Jordan.

The sisters met at Joseph's tent to tell all their kinsman goodbye before they marched to the area where they would be divided to serve under captains of hundreds and captains of thousands, and by what weapon they handled best.

After the men left, the women went to the commercial area to watch when all their men passed by in battle array. They spent the night—as did hundreds of other women and children who belonged to these soldiers.

Around noon the next day they began to hear cheers. Soon the men began to pass by, following their different standards. These were men from barely twenty up into the mid-fifties—all able bodied. Some, like Ariel and Helek, were veterans of other battles; some hadn't the least idea what might be in store for them.

They passed on by the women and children, each bearing their own weapon, or weapons. Some were singing their marching songs, some counted cadence together, some were waving and calling out to loved ones as they were recognized in the crowd. And then they were gone!

They were not to return home, except now and then on individual furloughs between the different campaigns in Canaan, for seven years.

The sisters did not get to see their loved ones march by. They may have been in the wrong place, or their men embedded in the marchers too deep to see. But the hearts of these young women thrilled to see all of the valiant men going off to secure the home God had promised His People.

Epilogue

Seven years later the five daughters of Zelophehad attended the formal allotment to both halves of their father's tribe. Some were given the land they asked for in the old Amorite kingdoms on the east side of Jordan; some received land as the other tribes on the west side in Canaan.

There to receive their father's inheritance were found Mahlah and her two sons and their father, Helek. Noah and her twin sons were there with a beautiful baby girl held by her proud father, Asriel. Standing close by them was Hoglah, her husband, a daughter, and a baby son. Then there were the two younger sisters attended by their husbands. Milcah and Tirzah had each produced a male child—sturdy little sons of Zelophehad.

About the Author

Author Wynell Brooks Hutson is a Bible teacher who resides in Hereford, Texas. She is an R.N., retired, and an artist who has taught classes in oil painting. This is the author's second novel and third published work. Her reason for writing this book is to fill out the few intriguing lines given in scripture and make it into a tale of what might have happened to bring the daughters of Zelophehad into their inheritance.